IZZY NEWTON AND THE S.M.A.R.T. SQUAD

THE LAW OF CAVITIES

VALERIE TRIPP

Illustrated by Millie Liu

UNDER THE *Stars*

NATIONAL GEOGRAPHIC

Since 1888, the National Geographic Society has funded more than 14,000 research, conservation, education, and storytelling projects around the world. National Geographic Partners distributes a portion of the funds it receives from your purchase to National Geographic Society to support programs including the conservation of animals and their habitats. To learn more, visit natgeo.com/info.

For more information, visit nationalgeographic.com, call 1-877-873-6846, or write to the following address:

National Geographic Partners, LLC
1145 17th Street NW
Washington, DC 20036-4688 U.S.A.

For librarians and teachers: nationalgeographic.com/books/librarians-and-educators

More for kids from National Geographic: natgeokids.com

National Geographic Kids magazine inspires children to explore their world with fun yet educational articles on animals, science, nature, and more. Using fresh storytelling and amazing photography, *Nat Geo Kids* shows kids ages 6 to 14 the fascinating truth about the world—and why they should care. **natgeo.com/subscribe**

For rights or permissions inquiries, please contact National Geographic Books Subsidiary Rights: bookrights@natgeo.com

Designed by Julide Dengel
Illustrations by Millie Liu

Hardcover ISBN: 978-1-4263-7302-2
Reinforced library binding ISBN: 978-1-4263-7304-6

Printed in the United States of America
22/WOR/1

For the Lunch Bunch:
Arsema, Baeza, Caroline,
Emily, Madelyn, Morgan, and Nora,
and their wonderful
teacher Emily Pacconi,
with love and heartfelt
gratitude forever.

–Valerie Tripp

For the gazillionth time, Izzy Newton ran her tongue across her teeth.

"New braces?" asked someone, plunking down next to her on the bus.

Oh, no, thought Izzy. It was Trevor Gawande. She really didn't want to look like a dorky metal mouth in front of him of all people. *Shake it off,* she told herself firmly. It was a sunny day in June, and a group of Atom Middle School sixth graders were boarding buses for their Outdoor Education trip. Izzy was determined to be calm and not worry about random stuff like her braces. She pressed her lips shut and nodded.

"I can see that you went for heavy metal, like I did," said Trevor. "When I had braces, I had so much metal in my mouth I was my own magnetic field. I was so wired, I could have generated enough electricity to light New York City."

Izzy couldn't help laughing. Then, quickly, she hid her mouth with her hand. "I was hoping for invisible braces," she said. "But they're too expensive, and they take longer, too."

"Yeah," said Trevor. He grinned. "I'm sure that your orthodontist gave you the scary speech about always using your headgear and rubber bands and bite plate and—"

"And how if I'm not super careful about brushing and flossing and using mouthwash, I'll get cavities in every tooth in my head," Izzy added. "And how serious getting those cavities will be."

"The gravity of cavities," said Trevor in a low, scary voice that made Izzy chuckle.

"I'm following the rules," said Izzy. "I just brushed my teeth in the bathroom after lunch. It was weird—and kind of gross."

"I bet," said Trevor. "I also remember that I wasn't supposed to eat anything too hot, too cold, too soft, too hard, too sticky, or too acidic. And nothing that required frontal attack, like corn on the cob or apples. That left pretty much nothing. Though I did swallow at least one mini rubber band a day."

Izzy laughed, and this time she didn't bother to cover her mouth. Trevor made it easy to talk about her braces, which was a relief. She dreaded kids teasing her about being a brace face. Dealing with the care of her brand-new braces on a camping trip was anxiety provoking enough. Izzy took a deep breath. She had worked *so* hard to be more confident over the past year, since the beginning of middle school. Outdoor Ed was going to be a test for her, a tough test. She'd be away from home, away from family, and away from school. Izzy knew that being in a completely unfamiliar place for three days would be a challenge, but she hoped that she could at least not spiral down into dizzy-Izzy-ness. That was her new mantra: *No dizzy-Izzy-ness.*

Being with her friends 24/7 would help. They were The Best. Charlie Darwin and Gina Carver were sharing a bus seat across the

9

aisle. *Probably talking about running,* thought Izzy. They were both on the track team. Or maybe they were discussing the rain catcher that Gina, who loved to tinker and engineer things, had built for Charlie's garden. Marie Curie and Allie Einstein were walking down the aisle of the bus. Marie, who loved both chemistry and fashion, tucked a green strand of hair behind her ear. Allie, who loved math and technology, was carrying her laptop, open and on. Izzy smiled, thinking about how she and her friends put their science smarts to use. They were best friends *and* they were a secret team called the S.M.A.R.T. Squad, which stood for **S**olving **M**ysteries **A**nd **R**evealing **T**ruths. The Squad

had solved a few mysteries at Atom Middle School this year, and Izzy had tucked the black-and-white composition book they used to record their mysteries in her backpack—just in case.

When Marie saw Trevor seated next to Izzy, she raised one eyebrow infinitesimally, but said only "Hi" and slid into the seat behind Izzy.

Allie, on the other hand, hooted when she saw Trevor. "Whoa, Izzy," she said, grinning hugely. "I guess *that* seat is taken!"

Izzy flushed. She groaned inwardly, thinking, *Just when I get a grip on one kind of embarrassment, a whole new universe opens up. Now Allie's going to tease me about Trevor—while he's sitting right next to me.*

But Allie switched her attention to Marie's hair. "Cool streak," she said as she sat next to Marie. "Did you dye your hair green in honor of Outdoor Ed?"

"Absolutely," said Marie, grinning. "Gotta go green. This trip is all about nature, right?"

"I guess," said Allie. "I prefer numbers. They don't sting or bite or give you a rash. They're never poisonous. Oh, that reminds me." Suddenly, Allie stood up. She clapped her hands, raised both arms, and hollered, "Hey! Everyone, listen up. I have an announcement."

Izzy would rather eat a bowl of live worms than call attention to herself. But Allie waved her hands and proclaimed to the busload of kids, "Okay, I'm going on record. I'm telling you right now: I will *walk* home from

11

Outdoor Ed if I see *one* snake."

Everyone laughed and clapped. A boy started stamping his feet and chanting, *"R-a-t-t-l-e-s-n-a-k-e spells rattlesnake, rattlesnake."* Soon all the kids joined in, and the bus shook with the noise.

When the commotion died down, Marie said, "No joke. Snakes creep me out, too, Allie."

"How about you guys?" Allie asked, whacking Trevor on the shoulder.

"Yeah, no, I'm with you on snakes," said Trevor.

"Me too," said Izzy, shuddering.

"Well," said Charlie. "Snakes *are* part of the food chain. Some snakes eat rodents. Others eat insects and slugs. And then raccoons, foxes, and coyotes eat snakes."

"Okay, that settles it," said Allie. "I don't like anything snakes eat or what they are eaten by, either. That day a copperhead sneaked into school was the worst day of my life."

"That wasn't a copperhead. It was a harmless baby northern brown snake," said Charlie. "It's easy to tell them apart because the pupil of the northern brown is rounded, while the pupil of the copperhead is a vertical slit, like a cat's pupil."

"I'll never see eye to eye with ANY snake, ever," said Izzy.

"Me neither," agreed Marie. She and Izzy fist-bumped in agreement. "I didn't use my locker for a week, I was so afraid that there'd be a snake hidden inside."

"They *do* like to hide in hollowed-out spaces," said Charlie. "And in warm, dark cavities like boots and—"

"Sleeping bags," said Allie, using hers to bonk Marie on the head and making her laugh.

Allie went on, "Whoever this guy Outdoor Ed is, I don't like him. I prefer Indoor Ed. I can be perfectly well educated about the outdoors by staying safely indoors." She sighed dramatically. "This is going to be a very long three days for me."

"Oh, no, Allie," said Charlie sincerely. "If you give Outdoor Ed a chance I'm sure you'll like it. We'll be hiking and swimming and being out in nature."

"My older brothers went to Outdoor Ed when they were in sixth grade," said Izzy. "They didn't mention any snakes. They really liked the hikes, the campfires, and the mess hall food."

"I'm not sure *that* proves anything," joked Gina from across the aisle. "Lucas and Joseph are not a valid scientific sample. Those guys would *eat* snakes if they were on top of a pizza."

"True," laughed Izzy. "Still moving even."

Just then, Principal Delmonico appeared at the front of the bus. "Sixth graders," he said. "May I have your attention? Quiet, please. Remember, it is a privilege to go to the Environmental Education Experience at Camp Rosalie Edge. You will be representing Atom Middle School. I know you will make us proud. What is our school rule?"

"Be kind!" shouted all the kids.

"Excellent," Principal Delmonico continued. "Stay safe. Your eighth-grade junior counselors are riding on the other bus. When you get to camp, listen to them. And obey your chaperones, like Ms. Martinez here." He stepped aside to allow Ms. Martinez to pass him and walk down the aisle.

Izzy managed to give Ms. Martinez a watery smile as she went by.

Trevor slid Izzy a sympathetic look. He knew all about Ms. Martinez and Izzy and their spotty history together. Izzy had a hard time in Ms. Martinez's Forensics class; making speeches and debating were Izzy's idea of torture.

Trevor nudged Izzy. "Hey," he said quietly. "No one's going to ask you to make a speech during Outdoor Ed. Who'd be your audience—a squirrel?"

Izzy laughed. "Well, everyone knows squirrels *are* interested in nutty speeches."

Trevor came right back with, "I've heard they also like a corny joke sometimes."

"Painful," said Izzy, shaking her head.

As the buses rolled down the highway and away from town, Izzy appreciated that Trevor was quiet like she was. He didn't talk too much or sing "This Is the Song That Never Ends," no matter how loudly or with what enthusiasm Allie sang right behind him. Instead, Trevor was quietly reading about images the HiRISE camera sent back to Earth from Mars.

"I'm into those Mars images, too," Izzy said. "Well, anything about planets and space travel, actually. I like

the fact that since Mars has less mass than Earth, its surface gravity is only about thirty-eight percent as strong. I tell my cat, Wickins, to eat up. On Earth he weighs ten pounds, but he'd weigh only 3.8 pounds if he went to Mars."

"This is why we need the STEM team you and your friends are trying to start at school," said Trevor. "We'd make a movie about your cat and call it *Wickins the Mars Cat: Changing the Laws of Gravity Into the Claws of Gravity*."

"He'd love that," said Izzy. "For a cat, he's a big ham."

Trevor laughed. Then he said, "You know, a year on Mars is 687 Earth days, which is about how long this bus ride seems. It feels like we left Atom weeks ago."

In reality, they arrived at Camp Rosalie Edge in two hours, Earth time. Izzy had pressed herself close to the window to see *everything* as the bus bumped along a rocky, sandy, narrow road that sloped gradually downhill. The road was bordered by fir trees and below them, scrubby bushes. Above and between the treetops, the sky was blue and cloudless. When the bus pulled into the clearing, Izzy saw the camp buildings and, beyond them, the sea stretching out to meet the sky at the horizon.

Camp Rosalie Edge was not fancy at all. The buildings were basic—simple and sturdy. They were painted white with green trim and had grayed cedar shingle roofs and gray stone foundations. Best of all was the camp's setting. It faced a sparkling ocean. Not far offshore, small islands dotted the water like green stepping-stones. Izzy knew that in the summer, Camp Rosalie Edge was a sleepaway camp, so it had cabins, a mess hall, playing fields, a rec hall, a swimming pool, and a boathouse. Izzy planned to explore every *building*, every *thing*, and every *inch* of Camp Rosalie Edge.

The buses stopped in front of the rec hall. As the students scrambled to gather their gear, a friendly-looking woman climbed on the bus. "Hello, Atom

Middle Schoolers," she said. "Welcome. I'm Dr. Tamaki, camp director. You'll meet the rest of the staff in a second. We're glad you're here, and we know you'll have a great Outdoor Education experience with us at Camp Rosalie Edge. We've got lots of activities planned for you. Right now, all sixth graders will be surrendering their electronics."

"Awww," all the kids groaned.

"Yeah, yeah, the No Phone Groan." Dr. Tamaki laughed. "I get that a lot. But there's no point in whining. You'll be too busy doing stuff in real life to be glued to your phones anyway. And reception is bad here. You're almost off the grid. Why do you think 'edge' is part of the camp's name?"

"Because being parted from our phones makes us edgy," one kid joked.

"What if we get lost in the woods or something?" asked another kid.

"An adult chaperone will always be with you," said Dr. Tamaki, "and all the chaperones will have satellite phones." Izzy knew satellite phones weren't limited to areas covered by cell tower signals because they relayed signals off satellites orbiting Earth. Dr. Tamaki turned to the grown-ups and said, "Adult chaperones, before you go to your cabins, come to the camp office to pick up your sat phones."

The students followed Dr. Tamaki off the bus. As they handed in their cell phones and laptops, Dr. Tamaki said, "Boys, follow your head counselor, Gus, who's waving to you. Girls, follow your head counselor, Rachel. They'll show you to your assigned cabins. Drop off your gear, freshen up, and we'll reassemble for a meeting in the rec hall in about fifteen minutes."

"See you later, Izzy," said Trevor, heading off toward the boys' cabins.

"Okay," said Izzy. She swung her pack over her shoulder.

Allie nudged Izzy hard and wrinkled her forehead in a frown that meant *Say more!*

So Izzy said, "See you" and waved a little bit.

"Oh, my *gosh*, Izzy," moaned Allie. "You're going to have to raise your effort quota *exponentially*. Like this." In a voice so loud she scared birds out of the trees, Allie hollered, "See you at the rec hall in a little while, Trevor!"

This time, it was Izzy who moaned.

Rachel, the girls' head counselor, set a fast pace as she led the way on an uphill path. Along one side of the path, facing the fields and the beach and the ocean, there were small, snug-looking cabins. Like the other camp buildings, they were painted white and green. Every cabin had a little porch shaded by a sloping roof in the front and a clothesline attached to the back. As Izzy trotted up the hill past the cabins, her pack bounced on her back, making the stuff inside *clink* and *slosh*.

"What do you have in there?" asked Charlie. "A mobile chemistry lab?"

"I wish," sighed Izzy. "It's nowhere near as fun as a lab. Though come to think of it, some of the stuff belongs in a lab. It's mostly products for my teeth. Braces are high maintenance. There's a big risk of tooth decay."

"Oh, yeah, I remember," said Marie. "I had braces when my family lived in Paris. In French, braces are called *appareil dentaire,* or usually for short, *b-a-g-u-e-s,* which is pronounced 'bog.' I remember thinking, *Yup, got that right. All this stuff for tin-grin upkeep sure does bog me down.*"

"I'm glad my braces are off," said Allie. "I used to have *two* toothbrushes, one regular size and one interproximal. That's the kind with the bristles arranged in a point, meant to clean in tight spaces."

"I've got those two toothbrushes with me," said Izzy. "Not to mention mouthwash, toothpaste, toothpicks, waxed dental floss, a mini-mirror, and little rubber bands. It's a bummer to have to bring all this stuff on a camping trip."

"And I thought *my* pack was overloaded," said Charlie. "I'll stop complaining." She jostled her pack on her back. "It's heavy because I brought lots of gear: my bathing suit, hiking boots, a flashlight, books to read, and overnight camping stuff like my sleeping bag and mess kit and water bottle. Oh, and I brought snacks."

Gina laughed heartily. "You guys usually tease me about how much stuff I carry around," she said. "This time, *I'm* the one who packed light. Although," Gina admitted, "I did bring my pillow."

Rachel led the girls to Cabin Two. "During summer camp, all of the cabins are used. But during Outdoor Ed, we use only a few. Here's your home sweet home," she said, adding breezily, "And here's a word to the wise: Mice love snacks. So do raccoons. If you don't want four-legged visitors, keep your snacks under wraps. Okay, see you later."

"Yeesh, *mice*," groaned Izzy after Rachel had left.

"Oh, don't worry," said Charlie with a twinkle in her eye. "Some snakes eat mice."

"Thanks," said Izzy. "I feel much better. Not."

Sunlight streamed in through the windows and made the cabin warm and cheery. There were three bunk beds framing an open space. Marie, Allie, and Izzy chose top bunks, claiming that they were superior because they were farther from bugs, mice, and their snake predators. Charlie and Gina chose bottom bunks because they had easy access. Izzy was glad that Charlie, a sound sleeper, was in the bunk below hers. She knew it was good to have a quiet person below, and one who wouldn't wake up if she climbed down to go to the bathroom in the middle of the night.

At the end of the cabin farthest from the door, there was a small separate room. Across from that, there was a room with two sinks, a shower stall, and a toilet.

Marie emerged from an inspection with a frown.

"Uh-oh," said Charlie. "My spidey sense tells me you are not pleased with the bathroom facilities, Marie."

"I am not," said Marie. "Hygiene alert. I am not going to take a shower the whole time we're here. The shower is clean, but there are crickets in there. Spiders, too. And I'm not even going to mention the rustic toilet. It's clean and it flushes, but it's out of another century, like maybe the nineteenth."

"The little separate room is for our adult chaperone, and that's probably Ms. Martinez, right?" said Gina as the rest of the Squad unpacked. "Who's the empty bunk for?"

"It must be for our junior counselor," said Charlie. "One of the eighth-grade girls."

"Speaking of eighth-grade girls," said Allie, "did you see that Miss Congeniality, Maddie Sharpe, is here?" Maddie Sharpe was an eighth grader who had dissed Izzy for wanting to be on the ice hockey team. She had been snooty about the STEM team the girls hoped to start, too. "Let's hope we don't have to deal with *her.*"

Right on cue, Maddie walked through the door of Cabin Two. Izzy and her friends shot one another looks of horror, and Izzy silently repeated her mantra: *No dizzy-Izzy-ness.*

Izzy was processing her shock and dismay when Maddie spoke up. She had clearly overheard Allie, because she said, "Surprise! Here I am, your worst nightmare."

"Oh," Izzy began. "Maddie, no, we're—"

But Maddie cut her off. "I'm not exactly delirious with joy about being in your cabin, either," she said. She swung her pack and several tote bags onto the last free bunk bed. "So, I have two things to tell you. One, let's just ignore each other, okay? And two, don't even *think* about touching any of my stuff." She dumped one more bag onto the bed and then left.

"Whoa," breathed Charlie. "Harsh."

"I know, right?" said Gina.

"Maddie brought more stuff than Izzy did," said Marie. "Why'd she bring so many clothes?"

"Maybe she spills a lot," giggled Allie.

"Maybe she has outfits to wear during that awkward post-pajamas and pre-dressed stage," joked Marie.

"*Shh*," warned Charlie. "She may hear you. She's right outside."

They could sure hear *her*. As a junior counselor,

Maddie was not required to turn in her cell phone, and the girls could hear her making a call to a friend.

"Hi," Maddie was saying. "I'm calling you from the Tiny Tots Department. I knew I'd have to sleep in a cabin with sixth graders, but guess what? One of them is that science-y girl who plays ice hockey and wants a STEM team. You know, that shrimp, Eeensie-Izzy."

Izzy bristled. She hated to be teased about being small.

Maddie went on, "Yeah, that girl and her pre-K friends. They're all in the cabin now, probably homesick, the babies."

Maddie's voice faded as she walked away.

"Babies?" repeated Gina in an irritated voice. "We should pull some classic camp trick on Maddie to show her that we're not pre-K. Too bad we don't have shaving cream to put under her pillow."

"*Eww,*" said Izzy.

"I could sprinkle cookie crumbs between her sheets to attract mice and raccoons," said Allie. "They'd be 'treats on sheets' for the four-legged critters."

"How about something low tech like short-sheeting

her bed?" said Marie. "My older sister taught me how."

"My brother taught me," said Gina. "Let's do it."

Izzy felt reluctant. "Uh, guys," she began, "I don't think that's a good idea."

"We don't have time anyway. Come on," said Charlie. "Let's go to the rec hall. Last one there is a rotten egg."

"Oooh, a rotten egg," Allie cooed. *"That* would be a good thing to put in Maddie's bed."

The five friends sat together on the floor of the rec hall. Maddie was sitting with the other junior counselors. They lounged in the back, slouched against the wall, their long legs extended. Izzy, waving to Trevor, caught Maddie's eye, but Maddie just sneered and looked away.

"Okay, listen up," said Dr. Tamaki, and the meeting began. First, Dr. Tamaki ran over the ground rules of safety and conduct: No hiking, swimming, or boating alone. None of the above after dark, unless supervised.

No raiding the mess hall. No damaging the cabins. "I think your Atom Middle School motto covers interpersonal behavior thoroughly," said Dr. Tamaki. "Let's hear it."

"Be kind!" hollered the kids.

Izzy wiggled uncomfortably. Her conscience squirmed when she thought about how unhappy she and her friends were about having Maddie in their cabin. They'd said stuff about her that was unkind, and thinking about tricking her wasn't kind, either. Izzy glanced at her friends, but they looked undisturbed. Izzy wished she could be as nonchalant as they were.

"Tonight after dinner, you will all help with cleanup. Later, we'll have a campfire, and you will each be expected to bring firewood," said Dr. Tamaki. "At the campfire, of course, we'll have all the usual traditions of songs, roasted marshmallows, and ghost stories."

"*Oooooooo,*" moaned the junior counselors from the back of the hall, in mock fear. They hissed like snakes, screeched like banshees, purred like cheetahs, and slapped their legs to make the ominous sound of flapping wings. Izzy saw Maddie point to her and the rest of the S.M.A.R.T. Squad girls while whispering to the junior counselor next to her, who nodded vigorously and smiled.

Izzy had a sinking feeling in her stomach. Quickly, she scolded herself, *Stop it. Remember, stay calm.*

As she listened to the junior counselors, Dr. Tamaki nodded. "I can see that some junior counselors, or JCs, remember the ghost stories from their own Outdoor Ed experiences," said Dr. Tamaki. Then she went on, "Tomorrow morning, we'll have Team and Trust Building Exercises. Then after lunch, you'll depart for your overnight camping trips. You'll canoe or kayak to one of the outlying islands. Your group gets to choose which island. Your choices are Green Island, Lady Gray Island, Sir Pent Island, Shell Island, and Isle of Pines. They're all equally lovely and unspoiled."

Campers turned to one another to discuss which island they might choose. As their happy murmurs filled the hall, Izzy noticed a sad look sweep across Dr. Tamaki's face.

That's odd, Izzy thought. *She looks unhappy. I wonder what's on her mind.*

But Dr. Tamaki's voice sounded steady as she said, "Okay, so your first assignment is to enjoy every minute. Your second assignment is to report to the waterfront, where your counselors Gus and Rachel will give you swim and boating tests. Don't worry: If you don't pass, you can hike and camp here on the mainland. Also, between now and dinner, please find firewood for the campfire and write a letter to yourself to mail home. Gus and Rachel will give you paper, pencils, and stamped envelopes. In the letter, write your hopes and goals for Outdoor Ed. You can go to your cabin for Quiet Bunk Time, or you can fan out and find a solitary spot. See you at the mess hall for dinner at six."

The girls had just stood up when Maddie bustled over and herded them toward the door, saying, "Let's go, Cabin Two-ers. That firewood isn't going to collect itself."

Gina rolled her eyes at Maddie's bossiness. But the Squad left the rec hall to do their assignments.

"Let's meet at the waterfront for our swim and boating tests after we write our letters and collect firewood," said Gina.

"Okay," the others agreed.

"Be careful when you're looking for wood," said Allie as they parted. "Watch out for snakes and bugs and poison ivy."

Izzy decided to write her letter first, and then look for wood. She went back to Cabin Two and picked up the Squad's composition book to have something solid to write on. Thinking that Ms. Martinez might appear at the cabin any minute, and not really wanting to see her, Izzy left and found a quiet spot at the edge of the beach, hidden behind a big rock. She sat with her back against it and wrote:

Dear Me,

My hopes and my goals for Outdoor Ed are to learn stuff about nature, take care of my braces, have fun with my friends (they are The Best), and my usual goal, to NOT freak out. Here are things to NOT spiral down into dizzy-Izzy-ness about:

Maddie, Ms. Martinez, tooth care, Trevor, and I guess that's all, except I really hope I don't run into any snakes, and that's the tooth.

Love, Me

Izzy addressed the envelope to herself and sealed her letter inside. Before she stood, she tilted her head back and closed her eyes, enjoying the breeze on her face. Just then, she heard Ms. Martinez's voice saying, "Is it definite then?"

Oh, no, thought Izzy. *I came down here on purpose so that I wouldn't bump into Ms. Martinez, and now here she is.*

Izzy stayed hidden behind the big rock. She heard Dr. Tamaki sigh deeply and say, "I'm afraid so. We've been threatened by this possibility before. But this time it looks like it's really going to happen, and happen soon. I can't think of any way to stop it."

"I'm so sorry," said Ms. Martinez. "It's a terrible shame, and such a waste."

"It's a loss to science," said Dr. Tamaki, her voice heavy with regret. "Not to mention the students who—"

Izzy couldn't hear the end of Dr. Tamaki's sentence because as Dr. Tamaki and Ms. Martinez walked away, their voices were swallowed up by the sound of rolling waves.

Quickly, Izzy opened the Squad's composition book and scribbled notes about what she had overheard.

... We are the JCs
Mighty, mighty JCs
Everywhere we go-oh,
People want to know-oh,
who we are
So we tell them ...

"Get a load of the lead singer of the junior counselors'—I mean the JCs'—rock band over there," said Allie, jabbing Izzy in the ribs. "It's Maddie."

"I kind of expected her to think all the camp-y stuff like singing at dinner was dorky," said Izzy. "But she loves it. She's, like, queen of the JCs' table."

"Go figure," shrugged Marie.

The girls were in the mess hall, eating dinner. They had all passed their swimming and boating tests easily.

Allie was especially good at boating. Her family had a house at Silver Lake, so she'd been canoeing and kayaking for years.

The food at dinner was pretty good, except for dessert, which was gelatin.

"You've got to be kidding me," said Charlie. She poked the red, yellow, orange, and green globs on her plate and made them wobble. "I didn't know they even sold this stuff anymore."

"Oh, sure they do," said Marie. "Sometimes I use it to dye my hair." She slurped a spoonful of green gelatin. "Chemistry rules."

"I'd go for red if I were going to dye my hair," said Charlie, "so I'd look like a woodpecker." She stood up and cleared her plates from the table. "Come on. The JCs are already in the kitchen washing the dishes. Let's go help them before Maddie comes and scolds us. She sure loves telling us what to do! Anyway, the sooner we finish kitchen duty, the sooner we can get ready for the campfire."

Normally, Izzy and her friends and the other sixth graders would sort of gripe about doing chores. But swept up in the spirit of Camp Rosalie Edge, they happily helped wash and dry the dishes, wipe the tables, sweep the floors of the mess hall, and put food away without complaining.

In a kitchen cupboard, Allie found packets of gelatin mix and waved a handful of green ones at Marie. "Need a touch-up?" she teased. "We've got a lot of green in here."

"No, thanks," laughed Marie. "Though I would rather use that for hair dye than eat it."

"Allie," said Maddie testily. "Put that gelatin mix back where it belongs."

"Yes, sir!" said Allie, saluting. She put the mix back with exaggerated care, as if it were explosive.

Izzy and Trevor had a race to see who could turn the most chairs over on top of the most tables fastest, so the job was soon done.

"Meet you at the campfire?" asked Trevor.

"I'll be there in an hour or two, after I finish my extensive after-dinner toothbrushing regimen," joked Izzy. "Gotta take care of the train tracks. Chew, chew, right?"

"Right," agreed Trevor as he headed toward the boys' cabins.

Ms. Martinez was waiting for the girls in Cabin Two. "Hello, Izzy," she said.

"Hi, Ms. Martinez," said Izzy. She introduced the rest of the Squad. "These are my friends. This is Charlie, Allie, Marie, and Gina."

"Hello," said Ms. Martinez. "It's nice to meet you. I know Izzy already."

"From Forensics class," Allie piped up. Izzy winced when Allie added, "Izzy's told us *all* about you."

"Yes, well, good," said Ms. Martinez briskly. "Now, be sure to bring a jacket to the campfire, everyone, and a flashlight. You don't want to fall down in the dark. I'll see you there."

After she left, Marie said, "She doesn't seem so bad, Izzy."

Izzy flushed. "She's not. I mean, I was such a total loss in Forensics first term that I earned that F in her class fair and square. She was pretty nice about it after, though. I just don't want to mess up this trip and lower her opinion of me again."

"Oh, Izzy," said Charlie kindly. "You are such a free-range worrier. It's like worrying is your default position. Everything is going to be fine during this trip. You'll see."

"I hope so," said Izzy. *Good old Charlie,* she thought gratefully. *She's always reassuring.* Izzy wondered if she should tell her friends about the worry that had been nagging at her ever since she'd overheard Dr. Tamaki and Ms. Martinez talking so seriously and unhappily at the beach.

But before Izzy said a word, Marie spoke up. "Come on," she said. She draped her jacket around her shoulders, looping the arms in front in a very chic way, so that she looked like a fashion model. "Hurry up. We don't want to miss the ghost stories."

"Not to mention the roasted marshmallows," added Allie as she tied her jacket around her waist so that it hung down like a very wide tail.

The girls used their flashlights to light their way as they walked down to the campfire site. Lamplight spilled out onto the path from the windows of Dr. Tamaki's office and lit the room within so well that the girls could see Dr. Tamaki at her desk. She was frowning as she spoke intently on the phone. Just as they passed by, she slammed her hand on her desk *hard*.

"*Whoa,*" said Charlie quietly. "Poor Dr. Tamaki. Looks like a bummer phone call."

I bet it has something to do with the conversation I overheard, thought Izzy.

At the campfire site, a bright fire was already burning, surrounded by pails of water and sand for safety. The campers had dropped off their firewood earlier, so there was a good-sized pile. Among the logs and bundles of kindling, Izzy spotted a few pieces of neatly sawed sticks. They were clearly machine cut

because though they were of different heights, they were uniform in length and width. Some were pointed at one end.

Gina saw them, too. "Look," she said. "Instead of logs, somebody brought pieces of surveyors' stakes."

"Oh, is that what they are?" asked Allie. "I found them tossed on the dirt, up near the road. There were longer ones, too, but they were stuck into the ground and had tags on them."

"It's a good thing you didn't pull those stakes out, Allie," said Gina. "I saw them, too. Surveyors put stakes like those in the ground to mark boundaries when they measure land."

"Measure land for what?" asked Izzy.

"Usually for developers to build on," said Gina.

"Maybe Camp Rosalie Edge is constructing new cabins or making the road wider."

"Whatever," said Allie. "Anyway, I'm glad the developers were throwing those stakes away. They were easy to get and nice and clean." She shuddered. "I didn't want to tromp through the undergrowth and risk touching poison ivy or stepping on a snake!"

"When Dr. Tamaki said we'd do all the old traditional campfire things, she wasn't kidding," Marie whispered to Izzy after they'd been at the campfire for a while.

Marie was right. First, they sang old songs, like "We Will, We Will, Rock You." Then they sang even older songs, like "Old MacDonald Had a Farm." Ms. Martinez did a mean rooster crow, but it was Trevor and the boys in his cabin who brought down the house with their donkey brays. Then the JCs and other counselors took turns telling ghost stories. The boys' head counselor, Gus, told a story about a man whose wife haunted him because he'd stolen her golden arm from her grave. Gus pretended to be the dead wife moaning to her husband, "Give me back my golden arm. Give me back my golden arm." Then Gus pretended to be the husband who was so terrified by his wife's ghost that he tossed her golden arm into the air and shouted, "TAKE IT!" The campers were so startled when Gus shouted that they jumped a foot!

Then they roasted marshmallows on long sticks. After they had eaten as many as they could, the JCs came around and collected their sticks.

"Must be a safety thing," Charlie murmured. The JCs tossed the sticks into the fire and then sat down behind the Squad.

"It's time for one last story," said Maddie. The fire crackled and filled the dark sky with sparks and smoke. Maddie held her flashlight under her chin so that her face looked spooky. She began to speak in a low, ominous voice. "Those old ghost stories are made up," she said. "But there's a story about Camp Rosalie Edge that lots of people believe is true. One of the outer islands is haunted. It's not haunted by a ghost, but by a

weird swamp creature that's part raptor, part snake, and all evil. A few years ago, on the darkest of dark nights, a group of sixth graders was sleeping out on one of the camp's islands.

One girl got out of her sleeping bag to get a drink of water. Suddenly, she heard a hissing sound, *Ssssst.* And then right by her ear, there was a *Screeeech* that made her blood run cold. The girl ran, but she couldn't get away from the huge creature. It flew so low over her that its sharp talons brushed against her shoulders, and she could smell its foul breath on her neck. As her friends watched in horror, the creature opened its powerful wings, swooped down, and GRABBED her."

As Maddie shouted "GRABBED," Izzy felt arms slither around her like snakes and squeeze the breath out of her. She heard a terrifying *"Screeeech"* in her ear, and then a shout of "GOTCHA!"

"Help!" shrieked Allie as Marie screamed, "Eeeek!" Even Charlie, who didn't scare easily, let out a loud yelp. Gina and Izzy slumped against each other and moaned, "Ohhhh." Other campers gasped and screamed, too. Izzy turned her head—and saw that it was the JCs behind them who'd grabbed the Cabin Two girls.

As her heart rate slowed back to normal, Izzy noticed that Trevor was looking at her with a worried expression. She gave him a wobbly thumbs-up to let him know she was shaken but okay.

Allie nudged Izzy and tilted her head toward Maddie. "She set us up," said Allie. "She's the snake in charge of the other snakes. Look."

Izzy looked at Maddie, who smiled a satisfied, sly smile and batted her eyelashes innocently, as if to say, *Who, me?*

After the heat and hot embarrassment at the campfire, the girls were glad the next activity was a night swim. Ms. Martinez had already left for the beach, so she was not in the cabin as the girls changed into their swimsuits, but Maddie flounced in.

"We know you told your friends to scare us at the campfire," said Marie crossly. She added with sarcasm, "Thanks. That was really nice of you."

"Oh," said Maddie with fake sympathy. "Was it too frightening for you little kids? Sorry. It's a brand-new Camp Rosalie Edge tradition we invented just for you."

"You really like camp traditions, don't you?" said Charlie. "In fact, you love all of this camp stuff."

Maddie shrugged.

"I assumed you came on this trip because you *had* to come," said Allie. "You know, for extra credit."

"Like because I flunked science and this is makeup?" said Maddie. "No, Allie. I may not be all about a STEM team like you nerds are, but I volunteered to come because I had a good time here on *my* Outdoor Ed trip when I was in sixth grade. Of course, I volunteered before I knew I'd be stuck in *your* cabin. Well, I plan to unstick myself as much as possible. Like right now, a bunch of us eighth graders are going to swim in the pool, not the ocean. Enjoy your sand and salt." And with that, Maddie flounced off again.

"I have to admit, I *was* scared," said Gina. "When the JCs grabbed us, it was like being strangled by a boa constrictor."

"It was *mean*," said Charlie. "I don't get Maddie. Our S.M.A.R.T. Squad should take *her* on. We should try to figure out why she does what she does. We can apply the scientific method and Solve the Mystery And Reveal the Truth about Maddie."

"My mother would say that she's having a bad attack of The Thirteens," said Marie. "My sister was the same way when she was thirteen." Only half-joking, she added, "My family's still getting over it."

"Well, *I* think we should short-sheet Maddie's bed," said Allie. "We need to get back at her."

"Oh ..." Izzy began.

But swiftly, the other girls moved Maddie's stuff off her bunk bed and onto the floor.

As she set Maddie's pack on the floor, Allie did a dead-on impersonation of Maddie. "Don't even *think* about touching any of my stuff," she said.

"Okay, Maddie," said Marie, with a giant wink. She

took off the blanket and untucked the top sheet. Neatly, she tucked the top sheet over the head of the mattress so that it looked as if it were the bottom sheet. Gina folded the sheet in half, bringing one end up to the pillow. Then she put the blanket back in place and folded the edge of the sheet over the top of the blanket. Marie tucked the blanket in all around, neat and tidy. Charlie and Allie put Maddie's stuff back on the bunk, arranged just as it had been before.

"Ta-da," Marie said. "Done."

"Maddie has been karma-fried," said Gina.

"What does that mean?" asked Charlie.

"I made it up," said Gina. "It means revenge for being mean. Maddie was mean to us, and now we've paid her back."

Izzy was hesitant. She began, "Are you sure—"

"Speaking of fried," said Allie, cutting her off. "I'm hot. Let's go jump in the ocean."

The waves were gentle and the water was comfortably cool. Some of the sixth graders had a splash fight. But Izzy and her friends floated peacefully, letting the water buoy and rock them. They floated for such a long time that they felt happily tired as they trudged back up the hill to Cabin Two.

As they entered the cabin, Ms. Martinez popped her head out of the door to her little room. "Good night," she said. "Don't stay up all night talking. Tomorrow's a big

day. You'll need to be sharp. And as the poet Maya Angelou says, 'Nothing will work unless you do.'"

"Okay," said Izzy. The others joined her in saying, "Good night, Ms. Martinez."

The girls brushed their teeth, put on their pajamas, and climbed into their bunks.

Marie flopped over onto her stomach and leaned down from her top bunk. "Let's spill the tea before Maddie gets back," she whispered. "So, Izzy, about Trevor: Is he still just a friend, or has he been promoted to boyfriend status?"

"He's a *friend*," said Izzy.

"But he's a *boy*," said Charlie.

"I'm familiar with the concept," said Izzy. "I do have two brothers, you know."

"Nope, nope," said Allie. "We're not falling for that. Brothers do not enter into this equation at all. We all saw you face-to-face with Trevor on the bus. What were you talking about?"

"Oh, Mars," said Izzy. "And a STEM team and braces and the gravity of cavities."

"How romantic," teased Gina. The other girls giggled.

"Hey," said Marie. "We shouldn't give Izzy a hard time. She and Trevor both like science, so they were probably talking about the physics, chemistry, and biology of braces."

"Say what?" asked Gina.

Patiently, Marie explained, "The physics is that the braces apply force to move the teeth in a certain direction. Then the body sends a chemical signal in response to that force, and that causes biological changes in the bone, which allows the tooth to move."

"Please tell me that is not what you talked about, Izzy," said Allie. "That would have been the boringest conversation *ever*."

"The most boring," Gina corrected.

"Right," said Allie. "What did you *really* talk about, Izzy?"

"Trevor was nice about what a total pain tooth care is when you have braces," said Izzy, "and how much stuff you need."

"You sure are well equipped mouthwise," said Marie.

"Yes, by gum, I am," punned Izzy, glad that the conversation had moved off the topic of Trevor and on to the topic of teeth.

The girls were quiet for a moment.

Izzy listened to the soft lull of the ocean in the distance.

Then Gina said a little nervously, "Those crickets sure are loud. And what's banging on the window screens?"

"Moths," said Charlie. "They're attracted to the light—"

"Which we have to leave on for Maddie," complained Marie.

"Some moths are attracted to light, and some moths are repelled by light," said Charlie.

"I'm repelled by whatever's in this mattress," said Allie. "It feels like it's stuffed with thorns, and it smells like it's stuffed with wet horsehair." She took a deep breath. "Oh, wait, no, that's my own hair I'm smelling."

The girls laughed softly, and Izzy said, "Go ahead and complain about crickets and moths and mattresses and smelly hair, but you can't fool me. I know that all of you like it here as much as I do. Even you, Allie, in spite of what you said on the bus."

"You're right," Allie admitted.

"Yes," said Charlie. *"Es verdad.* It's partly because we

are all here together. I mean, you guys are fun at home, but you're even more fun here."

"Camp's good," said Gina in her understated way. "I like it, and I like the people who work here."

"Me too," said Izzy. "So, I feel bad because something is really bothering Dr. Tamaki. I overheard her talking to Ms. Martinez at the beach, and now *she's* unhappy about whatever it is, too." Izzy pulled the S.M.A.R.T. Squad composition book out from under her pillow. "Look," she said.

The girls climbed out of their bunks. They stood squashed together next to Izzy and read her notes.

- Make an Observation: Dr. Tamaki looked unhappy at the rec hall meeting, and at the beach, she and Ms. Martinez sounded unhappy.
- Form a Question: What is bothering them?
- Form a Hypothesis: It has to do with the "terrible shame" and "waste" and "loss to science" that can't be stopped and will "happen soon."
- Conduct an Experiment: In this case, more data is needed before an experiment can be planned, so I'll look and listen for clues.
- Analyze the Data and Draw a Conclusion: To come!

"This sounds like a mystery for the S.M.A.R.T. Squad to solve," Charlie said eagerly. "We'll all 'look and listen for clues.'"

"Yes," said Marie. "We'll collect evidence, and we'll figure out what is bothering Dr. Tamaki and Ms. Martinez."

"Okay," Allie began. "I think the first—"

"*Shh!* Maddie's coming," Gina said. "Hide the book, Izzy."

Quickly, Izzy shoved the composition book under her pillow. All the girls scurried back to their bunks and pretended to be asleep.

Maddie turned off the light that had attracted the moths. But she lit her flashlight, so the girls could see her pull back the blanket on her bunk. They watched her struggle to get into her short-sheeted bed while they—all but Izzy, that is—struggled to suppress their giggles. After a few fruitless tries, Maddie wised up.

"Very funny," said Maddie fiercely but quietly, so as not to be heard by Ms. Martinez. She yanked her blanket and sheet off the bunk. "I have two things to tell you. First, short-sheeting my bed is just the kind of immature stunt I'd expect from you babies. Second, I know you did this to get back at me for the ghost-story trick. But watch out. This is *nothing*. I am way ahead of you when it comes to revenge."

"Revenge," echoed Marie in a scary, hoarse voice.

"*Sssss,*" hissed Allie, imitating Maddie's swamp creature. "*Whoosh.*"

"Gotcha," said Gina.

"Oh, *honestly!*" exclaimed Maddie. She plunked herself into bed and put the pillow over her head.

"We're even now," Izzy whispered to the Squad. "Let's not make Maddie madder."

"Okay," said Charlie cheerfully. "We don't want her to turn into a monster." But even Charlie could not resist one more "*Sssss.*"

4

"Yikes," whispered Izzy. She and the other S.M.A.R.T. Squad members were gathered around Maddie's bunk. Izzy was only half awake. Just seconds ago, Allie had shaken her shoulder, ordered her in an urgent whisper to get up, and then dragged her over to look at a very weird sight. Maddie was asleep. Her hair was spread down her back, and it was *green!*

"Do you think she dyed her hair last night?" Marie asked. "How—"

At that moment, Maddie woke up. She opened one eye. "Hey," she croaked when she saw the sixth graders standing around her. "What are you doing?"

"Nothing," said all five together.

"How come you're staring at me?" asked Maddie, suspicious. She dug into one of her many bags and pulled out a hand mirror. *"Greeeeeen!"* she shrieked when she saw her hair. "Green! What have you done to me? You dyed my hair!"

"We didn't do it," said Marie.

"Yes, you did," Maddie insisted. "My hair's the same seasick green as yours, Marie. And Allie, I saw you waving around those packs of green gelatin mix after dinner. I bet you took that mix from the mess hall and used it to dye my hair while I was asleep."

"I did *not*," said Allie.

"Calm down, Maddie," said Charlie. "Be reasonable."

But Maddie wasn't listening. She scrambled out of bed, shoved everyone out of her way, ran to the bathroom, stuck her head in the sink, turned the water on full force, and scrubbed. "Oh, it's not washing out," she wailed. "What'll I do?"

"What is going on?" asked Ms. Martinez, coming out of her room.

Maddie's wet face was tragic. "First they short-sheeted my bed," she said, "and now look what they've done. They've dyed my hair green, *permanently!*"

"Is that true?" Ms. Martinez asked. When no one spoke, she said, "Izzy?"

Oh, no, thought Izzy. *Here we go. Ms. Martinez is going to think less of me than ever.* "Well," Izzy admitted, "Maddie pulled a mean trick on us at the campfire, so we *did* short-sheet her bed for revenge. But—"

"Stop," said Ms. Martinez, holding up her hands. "I'm disappointed in you, *all* of you. I want this childish bickering to stop right now. Here you are, stirring up silly, unnecessary trouble when *real* trouble …" She stopped, and then went on, "We're going on an overnight tonight, and we have to function together as a team. So apologize to one another and move on."

"We didn't dye it," said Charlie. "But we're sorry your hair is green, Maddie."

Maddie was sullenly silent.

"Maddie?" said Ms. Martinez. "It's your turn to apologize."

"Apologize?" Maddie protested. *"They're* the ones who dyed *my* hair *green."*

"I don't want to hear it," said Ms. Martinez. She sounded tense and impatient. "You got yourselves into this mess. Get yourselves out." She left.

"Oh," huffed Maddie. She pulled her clothes on and hid her hair under a bandana. Before she stormed out, she said in a freezing-cold voice, "You guys think you're so smart. But you've blown it this time. You've really gone too far." She turned and looked directly at Izzy and said, "You can just forget about that STEM team thing you've been talking about all year. My mother is the head of the school board. I'll tell her to veto the STEM team idea, and she will." The door slammed shut behind her.

The five S.M.A.R.T. Squadders looked at one another with solemn faces.

"Wow," said Charlie softly. She shivered. "Maddie's like Medusa—you know, that Greek monster whose hair is green because it's made of snakes and if she looks at you, then you turn to stone."

Maddie herself certainly was stony at breakfast. The girls saw her talking to the other eighth graders at her table, frowning, pointing to their table and frowning harder, and then showing her friends a lock of her green hair from under her bandana. Everyone at her table gasped, and then turned furious faces toward the Squad.

"We're toast," said Marie as they walked back into their cabin after breakfast to get ready for their morning activities. "Maddie is bad-mouthing us. She's turning everyone against us."

"But we're innocent," said Gina. "I hate being blamed for something I didn't do."

"Me too," Charlie sighed. "But we shouldn't gang up and be mean like Maddie and her friends. I don't like this whole karma-fried idea."

"Me neither," said Izzy, as she flossed her teeth. "In spite of everything, I do feel sorry for Maddie. *We* didn't dye her hair green, but *some*thing did."

"I think," said Allie, "that there is a confounding variable at work here."

"What's that?" asked Marie.

"Well, it's a math thing. An independent variable is the cause, and a dependent variable is the effect," Allie explained. "But sometimes there's a third variable that might seem random, but is actually having an impact on the outcome, or the effect. Like, someone might say that eating an ice-cream cone makes you sweaty, but the confounding variable is that you usually eat ice-cream cones in the summer, when you also get sweaty. In our case, Maddie thinks we did something to cause her green hair, which is the effect. I think the thing that made Maddie's hair green is a confounding variable that we're just not seeing."

"Like what?" asked Gina.

Nobody had an answer.

"Let's be scientific about this," said Izzy. "None of us woke up with green hair. Well, Marie has a green *streak*, but she dyed that streak deliberately, days ago. What did Maddie do that none of us did last night?"

"Maybe she ate something weird at dinner," said Gina.

"Nothing anybody ate would make their hair turn green," said Charlie. "Not even too much green gelatin."

"Maybe she took a shower in our ancient bathroom and the water dyed her hair," said Izzy.

"I took a shower and nothing happened to my hair," said Allie. "The water's fine."

"Hey," said Marie. "We swam in the ocean last night, but Maddie swam in the pool with the other eighth graders, right?"

"Right," the girls agreed.

"Maybe there was too much chlorine in the pool water," said Marie. "That would make the water acidic, which could make hair turn green."

"How?" asked Izzy.

"Pool water contains chlorine to get rid of stuff like germs," said Marie. "Pool water can also have copper in it. If there's a lot of chlorine in the water, the water gets acidic. When copper and chlorine form bonds—that means they stick together—they make a kind of sticky green film that gloms onto the proteins in hair and … bad news, the hair turns green."

"Then why didn't ALL the eighth graders get green hair?" asked Gina.

"All the other eighth graders on this trip have dark hair," said Izzy. "Maddie is the only one with blond hair, so that's probably why hers is the only one that shows the green."

"Can Maddie ever get the green out?" asked Charlie.

"Yes," said Marie. "Her hair will return to its normal color after she washes it with a special kind of shampoo, called a chelating shampoo."

"Uh-oh," said Izzy. "So until we go home and Maddie can get some chelating shampoo, she'll be stuck with green hair? I sure don't want to be the one to tell her *that*."

"If your theory is true, how do we prove it—and our innocence?" asked Allie.

"You've got blond hair, Allie," said Gina. "You could swim in the pool and see if your hair turns green."

"No, thanks," said Allie. "I mean, no offense, Marie, your green streak is cool. A whole head of green hair is not. Look at Maddie. Anyway, it would only make things worse. Maddie would think I was making fun of her if I had green hair, too. She's always so *extra*. She'd *explode*."

"A hair-raising image," punned Izzy. She couldn't help herself.

"You don't have to dye your whole head, Allie," said Charlie. "Just cut off a chunk of hair and put it in a baggie of pool water and leave it overnight."

"Ohhhh-kaaay," said Allie. "I'll do that. But Maddie

doesn't trust us. I bet she'll think we dyed my hair with gelatin mix just to trick her. And what if the pool water problem has been fixed by now so that it does *not* turn my hair green? I think we'd better find another way to prove to Maddie that her hair is green because of the chlorine and copper in the pool water."

"Allie, you're a genius," said Marie. "We can turn pennies green. Pennies contain copper. White vinegar is an acid, just like chlorine when it's added to water. So we get some pennies and then we borrow some white vinegar from the mess hall. We pour the vinegar on the pennies and then we wait. With any luck, by the time we return from our overnight trip, the pennies will be green. We can explain to Maddie how that's kind of what happened in the pool water to make her hair green."

"It'll be best to use pennies made before 1982," said Gina. "Back then, pennies were ninety-five percent copper and five percent zinc. In 1982, they became 97.5 percent zinc and 2.5 percent copper. Really, just copper-plated zinc."

"Science to the rescue once again," Charlie said,

grinning. "Maddie's green hair will be *another* mystery for the S.M.A.R.T. Squad. Write it in our notebook, Izzy."

"Okay," said Izzy. She pulled out the Squad's composition book from under her pillow, flipped to a clean page, and wrote:

- Make an Observation: Maddie's hair is green.
- Form a Question: Is the pool water responsible for turning it green?
- Form a Hypothesis: The pool water is too acidic.
- Conduct an Experiment: Put a lock of Allie's hair in a container of pool water. And as backup proof, pour white vinegar on copper pennies.
- Analyze the Data and Draw a Conclusion: ???

"Good thing none of the morning activities involve swimming in the pool," said Marie as the girls filled a baggie with pool water. "No one else will run the risk of green hair."

Charlie, who had brought nail clippers from the cabin, cut off a lock of Allie's hair.

66

Allie dropped her hair into the pool water and sighed with exaggerated sorrow, "Goodbye, my good old hair. You and I had lots of good times together, but now you are being sacrificed to science and to justice."

Gina ran back to Cabin Two to put the baggie in a safe place.

When everyone had gathered at the playing fields, Izzy saw that Maddie's green hair was well hidden beneath her bandana. If she felt any less angry, she was keeping that well hidden, too. She ignored Izzy and the rest of the Squad, mostly. When forced to interact, Maddie frowned and acted as if they were invisible and inaudible.

"I'm going to go out on a limb here and predict that Maddie is not going to take Ms. Martinez's advice and apologize to us," said Gina wryly.

"Ya think?" agreed Allie.

Izzy tried not to worry about the Maddie situation. She was already kind of stressed out about the activities. New things often intimidated her. It had taken her a whole summer to get up her nerve to jump off the rope swing into the lake, for example. Right now, Izzy muttered her mantra, *No dizzy-Izzy-ness.* She added, *Don't let Maddie bug you.*

During the introduction to the morning's Team and Trust Building Exercises, Maddie stayed as far away as possible from the Squad.

"Maddie's not interested in building a team *or* trust with us," said Gina.

"She treats us like we're some kind of invasive species of weeds," Charlie muttered.

"Well, look on the bright side," said Izzy. "At least she's not in our face."

"No, but she's in our *race,*" said Marie. "And that might be bad."

Marie was right. The first team-building exercise was a relay race, and the campers in every cabin were a team. Maddie, as the JC in Cabin Two, was part of the Squad's relay team, unfortunately. Word had it that the girls in Cabin Three were pretty fast. And before the race, the boys in Cabin Seven swaggered around bragging that they'd win. But Gina and Charlie were the fastest runners in the sixth grade—well, all of Atom Middle School, really—so Cabin Two won easily. Surprisingly,

Maddie ran her leg of the relay pretty well. Not in record speed, but respectably fast.

"I was afraid she'd run in slo-mo," said Marie, "just to spite us."

"I guess she knows that speed equals distance divided by time," joked Izzy. "And she wanted to keep her time with us short."

"No," said Charlie thoughtfully. "She won't say so, but I think Camp Rosalie Edge and its traditions matter to Maddie. She wants to do well here. Or anyway, she doesn't want to look like a loser, even if it means she has to help us. She cares about how she does in competitions here because she cares about camp."

Maddie may have cared about camp, but she made it clear that she didn't care whether or not anyone in Cabin Two liked her. During the second exercise, which was intended to build trust through teamwork, Gina had to navigate an obstacle course while

blindfolded. The rest of the Cabin Two crew was stationed at the obstacles along Gina's path so that they could call out directions. Everything went fine until Gina came to where Maddie stood.

"GO LEFT, GINA!" hollered Maddie at the top of her lungs. "Left, left, *left!*"

"Oh-*kay,*" said Gina, so rattled that she stopped. "You don't have to scream at me."

"GO!" screamed Maddie, louder than ever.

After completing the course and coming in second, Gina ripped off her blindfold. "Thanks for your help, Maddie," she said sarcastically. "Your gentle guidance really helped me."

Maddie shrugged, turned up her nose, and sauntered away.

Relations with Maddie sank still further during the next exercise: trust falls.

The sixth graders were the fallers, and their eighth-grade JCs were the catchers. Allie was supposed to go first, but she balked. "You're asking me to stand on a rock and fall backward into Maddie's arms?" she said to the rest of the Squad. "That is the worst idea I have ever

70

heard in my whole life. She thinks I'm a gelatin-sneaking, hair-dyeing creep. No way."

"But Allie," said Marie. "If you don't do the trust fall, you'll be confirming Maddie's idea that we're babies. She'll blab to everyone that we're not only mean pranksters; we're chickens, too."

"Hey, I'd rather be a chicken than Humpty-Dumpty, who had a great fall," said Allie. "You do it."

"No, thanks," said Marie. "I'd prefer wrestling a snake."

"I'll do it," said Izzy, to keep the peace. She walked over to Maddie and stepped up onto the rock.

"Oh, look at you, Eeensie-weensie-Izzy, acting all brave," said Maddie. "Ready?"

Izzy nodded. She turned her back toward Maddie, held her breath, and with a terrible sense of foreboding, fell backward.

But Maddie caught her safely.

"Thanks for catching me," said Izzy when she was on her feet again.

Maddie made a pretend confused face. "Oh, was that you? TBH, you're so little, I thought a feather fell into my arms."

"I know I'm small," said Izzy crossly. "You don't need to remind me."

Maddie smirked as if she was glad she'd irritated Izzy.

This irritated Izzy even more.

Luckily, the next activity was an egg-and-spoon race, and everyone got to choose a partner. Maddie immediately chose another JC. Before Izzy had a chance to ask a friend from the Squad, Trevor appeared.

"Hey," he said. "Want to be partners?"

"Okay," said Izzy.

"Solid," said Trevor with a lopsided grin.

"Don't say I didn't warn you," said Izzy. "I mean, who's a better partner in an egg-and-spoon race than someone named Newton—as in Newton's Law of Universal Gravitation. Egg? Spoon? Race? Gravity? What could go wrong? Plus, I'm a famous butterfingers. *Really* clumsy."

"Whoa," said Trevor, pretending to look stern. "Please don't speak that way about a friend of mine."

Izzy laughed. "You mean me dissing myself?"

"Yeah," said Trevor, nodding. "I do."

Izzy laughed again. "Okay," she said. "I'll zip it." She

drew her thumb across her lips, pretending to seal them shut, which made Trevor laugh.

They didn't win the race, but then again, no one won. No team's egg survived. Izzy felt pretty cheery as she helped scoop up the broken eggs, but her heart sank when the last activity was announced.

"To practice paying careful attention to team members' body language and unspoken communication, we're going to play charades," said Rachel, the girls' head counselor.

Oh, no, thought Izzy. Her least favorite thing—even worse than snakes—was standing up in front of people.

All of the Squad members sent her sympathetic looks, but Maddie pounced, losing no time in needling her.

"Uh-oh, Eeensie-Izzy," Maddie teased. "You don't have your cute little hockey uniform to hide behind here."

"Oh, was that you?" asked a kid who had overheard Maddie. "You're the one who wore your hockey uniform when you made a speech in Ms. Martinez's Forensics class? My friend told me about that. He said it was awesome."

"It was," said another kid. "I was there, in that class." She said to Izzy, "But I liked it even better the time you said that hockey was your 'spavorite fort.' That was the funniest thing that happened in Forensics class all year. Totally brilliant."

"Thanks," said Izzy modestly. Of course, her "spavorite fort" tongue tangle had felt humiliating and not at all brilliant at the time. Wearing her uniform while making a speech had been a desperate measure, taken because she was failing Forensics. Who'd have guessed that her classmates would think her blooper was a cool joke, a joke that she'd made on purpose?

Izzy saw Maddie yank her bandana down lower on her forehead and scowl, clearly annoyed that her teasing had backfired.

On the way to lunch, the girls stopped at the camp shop that sold bug repellent, flashlight batteries, and sunscreen. They traded two quarters for 50 pennies. Of those, six were dated before 1982. At the mess hall, Marie borrowed a bottle of white vinegar, some paper towels, and a baggie from the kitchen. Then she joined the rest of the girls at their table.

"If I had to predict which cabin is going to function worst as a team on the overnight, it would be us, Cabin Two," Allie said. "Because of Maddie. If you were plotting the possibility for conflict statistically, your confidence interval would be about, oh, infinity."

Charlie looked up from a salad as big as a farm and asked, "What's a 'confidence interval'?"

"It's another way to express probability," said Allie. "It's a range of values that you're pretty sure your true value is going to lie in. So I'm infinitely confident that Maddie is going to cause some sort of hot mess."

Charlie nodded, her mouth full.

"We might have a slim chance of working well as a team if we could prove our innocence to Maddie *before* the overnight," said Izzy.

"We can't," said Marie. "Allie's hair and the pennies need a while to turn really good and green. We can't hurry science. But we had better hurry lunch. We don't have much time to set up the experiment before we have to be at the dock to leave for the overnight. Eat fast."

They gulped their food and ran back to Cabin Two. Marie lined up the six pre-1982 pennies on a paper towel. "Here goes," she said. She poured white vinegar over the pennies.

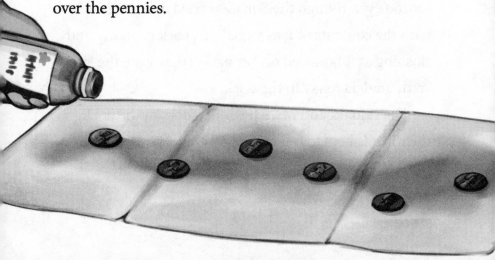

"P.U.," said Gina, recoiling. "That vinegar smells gross."

"Sure it does: It's acetic acid," said Marie. She folded the paper towel over the pennies, put them in the baggie, and then put it all on the bathroom windowsill next to the baggie of Allie's hair-in-pool water.

"Go green, you guys," Izzy encouraged the hair and the pennies. She crossed her fingers on both hands and held them up. "You'll prove our innocence. Let's hope."

"Let's *move*," said Allie, "or we'll literally miss the boat."

Izzy's big overnight pack was ready, but it took a while for her to gather up in her small daypack all the things she had to bring for her mouth and teeth and braces care. At the last second, she slid the S.M.A.R.T. Squad composition book and a pencil into her daypack, too. So even though the Squad hurried down the hill— with the contents of Izzy's small daypack clanking and sloshing as it bounced on her back—they were the last sixth graders to get to the dock.

Dr. Tamaki and Ms. Martinez stood on the dock, their heads bent together over a piece of paper. They were studying it so intently that they didn't look up.

But Maddie glared at the latecomers. She put her hands on her hips. "Nice of you to show up," she said.

Maddie spoke in an extra-loud voice, which made Ms. Martinez look up. She didn't say anything, but she sighed a heavy sigh.

Uh-oh, thought Izzy. *Did Ms. Martinez's opinion of me slide down a notch again because we're late? Or did she sigh because of what is written on the paper?*

"Okay, Cabin Two," said Dr. Tamaki in a no-nonsense manner. She shoved the paper in her pocket. "Because you're last, the only islands left to choose from are Lady Gray Island and Sir Pent Island. Which one will it be?"

"Lady Gray Island," said Maddie officiously. "That's where I went when I was in sixth grade, so that's where we'll go today."

"No," said Allie, quickly contradicting Maddie to show her that she could not boss the Squad around. "Dr. Tamaki, we'd like to go to Sir Pent Island, please. Right, girls?"

"Right," said the rest of the Squad firmly. They were

equally eager to stand up to Maddie.

Dr. Tamaki looked a little surprised. "Uh, okay, good," she said. "You'll have it to yourselves tonight. Actually, nobody's chosen to spend the night there for a while. It's the most remote island."

Maddie tilted her head. "And rumor has it that's where the swamp creature is," she said.

"We don't believe in your swamp creature, Maddie," said Gina. "Probably most campers just don't want to paddle as far as Sir Pent Island. But we don't mind, do we?"

"No," said Izzy, Charlie, Marie, and Allie.

As they all put on their life jackets and helmets, Dr. Tamaki asked Ms. Martinez, "Got your satellite phone?"

Ms. Martinez patted her daypack. "In here," she said.

"Good," said Dr. Tamaki. She turned to the campers. "Okay, we'll have Ms. Martinez, Marie, and Gina lead in the canoe," she said. "Maddie and Allie, you'll follow in the blue kayak. Charlie and Izzy, you'll bring up the rear in the red kayak."

Dr. Tamaki helped Ms. Martinez load the cooler of food into the canoe. As she bent forward, the paper that

Dr. Tamaki had pushed into her pocket fell out onto the dock. It fluttered open and a gust of wind lifted it, sending it scudding down the dock.

Allie chased the paper and caught it before it flew into the water. She handed it back to Dr. Tamaki.

"Thank you, Allie," said Dr. Tamaki. This time she folded the paper carefully and tucked it deeply and safely into her pocket.

"You're welcome," said Allie.

"Have a safe trip," said Dr. Tamaki as she left. "See you first thing tomorrow. Everyone's due back shortly after dawn."

Allie turned to Maddie and said, "Ship ahoy, Captain." She gestured toward the blue kayak. "Which end of this thing do you get in?"

Maddie squinted at Allie. "Are you telling me that you've never kayaked before?" she asked.

"Well, I kayaked yesterday, for my boat test," said Allie cheerfully. "But tell me again: Which end of the oar do I hold?"

"First of all, it's a paddle," said Maddie. "And you hold it in the middle."

"No kidding," said Allie.

Charlie and Izzy looked at each other. They both knew that Allie was pulling Maddie's leg. Allie knew all about kayaking. She had passed her boating test yesterday with flying colors.

"I have a sinking feeling about the Good Ship Maddie-and-Allie," Izzy whispered.

Charlie nodded vigorously. "Me too."

"Which hole do I sit in?" Allie asked Maddie.

"They're called cockpits," said Maddie. "You sit in the bow."

Allie gave her a blank look. "The what?"

"The bow's the front," snapped Maddie. "You take the front."

As she climbed in, Allie deliberately banged her paddle hard against the side of the kayak so that it made a loud crashing sound. "Oops, my bad," she said.

"Oh, *honestly*," said Maddie. "No! Put your legs out in front of you. Don't squash up like that."

Allie turned and waved her paddle at Charlie and Izzy. "Anchors aweigh," she said. "Maddie and I are on our way to the Bad Kayakers' Convention to pick up our

Lifetime Achievement Award for the All-Time Worst Kayakers Ever. See ya."

But before Allie had taken even one stroke, Maddie, boarding nimbly, commanded, "No joking in a boat, *ever*. And don't slap the water with your paddle or it'll splash all over me."

"Aye, aye, Captain," said Allie. As the blue kayak lurched forward in the water, Allie made a goofy face at Izzy and Charlie. They shook their heads and sighed at Allie's pretend ineptitude. *Typical Allie*, thought Izzy. *She always goes overboard. Let's hope not literally, in this case.* Izzy knew that Allie was only tricking Maddie to make her friends laugh. Izzy and Charlie paddled their red kayak close behind, to keep a careful eye on Allie and Maddie. Izzy saw that though Allie splashed a lot, like all good boaters she never did anything dangerous.

It was a perfect June day. The sun danced on the water, especially on the spray that Allie swept up with her paddle and deliberately showered upon Maddie behind her. Allie began to sing:

Row, row, row your boat
Off to Sir Pent Isle.

Merrily, merrily, merrily, merrily,
Splashing all the while.

Somehow, despite Allie's wacky-splashy paddling style, they arrived safely at Sir Pent Island after a long row.

"That was fun," said Allie, bubbling with fake enthusiasm as she bounced out of the blue kayak.

"For you, maybe," said Maddie. "I'm soaking wet. I couldn't be any wetter if I'd *swum* here."

"Oh, gosh, *really?*" said Allie, eyes wide.

"I don't know how you ever passed your boating test," Maddie huffed. "On the return trip to camp, you can ride in the canoe."

"Okay," said Allie cheerfully. She grinned at her friends as if to say, *Goal of irritating Maddie by faking kayak incompetence? Mission accomplished.*

Izzy gave Allie a thumbs-up signal followed by a time-out signal to say, *Okay, but no more teasing Maddie.*

The campers and Ms. Martinez dragged the kayaks and the canoe far up onto the beach, well away from the water's edge, and pulled them into a copse of scrub trees to the right of an enormous rock.

As they took their gear out of the boats, Ms. Martinez said, "You can leave your big packs. Just carry your daypacks, water, and snacks for our hike. We'll come back here later to set up camp for the night."

The mess hall staff had packed dinners and breakfasts for the overnight in a cooler. Now, with Maddie's help, Ms. Martinez put the cooler underneath the overturned canoe.

"Are you hiding the food to protect it from bears or something?" asked Marie.

"No," said Ms. Martinez. "It'll stay cooler under the canoe and in the shade cast by the trees and that big rock."

Gina tilted her head back and surveyed the rock, which loomed over them. The front part of the rock came to a sharp angle that pointed toward the water. "I dub thee 'Mount Shipshape,'" said Gina, "because your front sticks out toward the water like the prow of a ship."

"There's a narrow strip of beach for us to walk on between Mount Shipshape and the water now," said Izzy. "It's low tide. But we'd better return from our day hike before high tide. I bet during high tide the water comes all the way up to Mount Shipshape's prow, maybe even

86

past it. It will cover up the strip of beach and cut us off from our stuff."

"And our dinner," added Charlie.

"Don't worry," said Ms. Martinez. "We should be back well before the tide comes in." She shouldered her daypack. "I've got first aid equipment, energy bars, the satellite phone, a flashlight, water, and maps in here. So we're all set."

"Ms. Martinez has almost as much stuff in her pack as you do in yours, Izzy," said Maddie, softly so that only Izzy could hear. "You've brought your mobile dentist's office. I can hear it clanking."

"Mm-hmm," said Izzy. She wished she could come up with a clever joke like Trevor's about the gravity of cavities, but all she could think of to say was, "I have to brush my teeth even if all I eat is a snack."

Maddie closed her eyes and shook her head as if it were all too boring to endure.

Ms. Martinez said, "Okay, listen up. Our first activity is called Fine Feathered Friends. We'll be walking along the beach, staying near the shore. Keep your eyes out for found feathers, bird prints in the sand, and birds. Here are charts to help you identify any feathers or bird prints you find. And here's a chart of all the birds known to live on Sir Pent Island. Dr. Tamaki told me that the main campus and these islands are so pristine that there hasn't even been a full biological survey of the plants and animals living in them. And now it's too late, because soon—" Ms. Martinez shook her head, recalibrated, and said briskly, "Well, see how many birds you can spot. Stay within sight of me at all times." As she handed out the charts, she said, "Have fun."

What was Ms. Martinez talking about when she said, "And now it's too late, because soon …"? Izzy thought. *Is something bad going to happen to camp and the islands? Is that what's upsetting her and Dr. Tamaki?*

The girls walked single file along the strip of beach between the pointed base of Mount Shipshape and the water. Once Mount Shipshape was behind them, they saw a long sandy shore stretching ahead. Maddie strode

determinedly away by herself, bird chart in hand, but Ms. Martinez and the Squad strolled slowly in a group, pointing out shells to one another. Sometimes a wave surprised them and they had to run up the beach, squealing, to avoid getting their shoes soaked, which happened pretty soon anyway. They stopped often, as one girl or another knelt down in order to look at and identify bird prints in the sand. Whenever someone found a feather, they compared it with their chart to try to identify what kind of bird it came from and whether the bird was an adult or a baby. Often, Izzy saw Maddie's footprints and knee prints in places where she, too, had knelt to look closely at prints in the sand.

Graceful gulls swooped and dove. The white-capped waves curled, hit the shore with a splash, and slid up the beach and back down again. The air was scented so strongly with the salty smell of the ocean that Izzy could taste it.

Gradually, the beach curved gently to the right. After a while, Mount Shipshape was no longer visible behind them. When they had walked for an hour or so, Allie asked Ms. Martinez about stopping for a water break.

"Sure. I'll catch up with Maddie, and we'll wait for you," said Ms. Martinez. Maddie was so far ahead that she was just a speck on the horizon. "We can have our break together."

"Okay," said Allie, politely but without enthusiasm at the idea of being with Maddie.

The Squad continued to walk as Ms. Martinez jogged away. Gina said, "I'm glad Ms. Martinez is feeling better."

"What do you mean?" asked Marie. "Ms. Martinez hasn't been sick, has she?"

Gina shrugged. "All I know is that when I ran back to Cabin Two this morning with the baggie of Allie's hair in the pool water, I heard Ms. Martinez tell Rachel that she felt terrible."

"Maybe she meant unhappy, not sick," said Izzy.

"Well, whatever was in that letter that Dr. Tamaki showed Ms. Martinez on the dock sure didn't make her feel better," said Marie. "That letter seemed to upset them both."

"Oh, that wasn't a letter," said Allie. "When I handed it to Dr. Tamaki, I saw it was covered with numbers and shapes. I'm pretty sure it was a cadastral map."

"An astral map?" asked Izzy. "You mean like a map of the stars?"

"No, a *cad*astral map," said Allie. "A plat. You know, a plat is a plan that shows the dimensions of a property, drawn to scale. Usually, a plat shows how a piece of land is going to be divided up before buildings or roads or fences are going to be constructed on it."

Izzy stopped short. "Allie," she said slowly. "Did you see … did you see any *words* on the plat?"

Allie stopped short, too. She looked stricken. "Oh," she said. "Now that you mention it, I saw the words 'Camp Rosalie Edge' at the bottom."

Now the rest of the girls looked stricken, too. They stared at one another with horrified faces as they all realized the same thing: It seemed as if they had solved the mystery of what was upsetting Dr. Tamaki and Ms. Martinez, and it was something truly terrible.

Charlie was the first to say it aloud. "The surveyors' stakes and the plat can lead to only one conclusion: Camp Rosalie Edge is going to be divided up and developed, and it'll probably happen soon."

Izzy hated to add to the doom and gloom, but she had to say, with urgency, "And I heard Dr. Tamaki say that it is going to happen soon."

"Well," said Marie briskly. "As usual, solving one mystery has led straight to another. Now that we know what is bothering Dr. Tamaki and Ms. Martinez, our next S.M.A.R.T. Squad mystery has to be: Can Camp Rosalie Edge be saved?"

"Okay, lightning-round brainstorm time," said Gina. "Everybody kneel down and pretend we're identifying a bird track, in case Ms. Martinez or Maddie looks back at us." When all the girls had knelt, Gina said, "Right off the top of your head, give ideas for how to save the camp. I'll go first. We could save this place if we found a good reason for why it has to be protected, why it *can't* be developed. Like, let's say we found dinosaur bones, or rare fossils."

"Or wildlife—like an endangered animal," said Charlie, excitedly, "or a rare plant, like a special kind of orchid."

"Or an animal habitat, or a natural feature, like underground caves," said Izzy. "Or a source of natural energy, like wind power."

"Or something human-made, like graves or artifacts or remains of structures that should be in the National Register of Historic Places," said Marie.

"I don't know," said Allie. "What are the chances that we'll discover a phenomenal phenomenon that no one else has discovered? Plenty of people have been here before us."

"Yes," said Izzy, "but they were *not* us. They weren't the S.MA.R.T. Squad. We Solve Mysteries And Reveal Truths, remember? In this case, we'll reveal a truth that will solve the mystery: Can Camp Rosalie Edge be saved?"

"Let's hope the answer is yes," said Charlie. "And we had better start looking for that phenomenal phenomenon now, right here on Sir Pent Island. There's no time to lose. We'd also better join Ms. Martinez and Maddie. Come on."

Izzy and her friends were quiet. Izzy knew that they were all thinking hard—and hoping hard—as they hurried toward Ms. Martinez and Maddie.

When they caught up and the whole group was

together, they sat on the beach facing the
sparkling sea and drinking from their
water bottles.

"Hey," said Charlie. "Let's have a snack
with our water." From her pack she pulled
a bag of kale chips. "Plenty for everyone."

"I brought Bubbie's chocolate chip cookies," said
Allie. She passed the bag. "Have as many as you want."

"Thanks," said Charlie, Izzy, Marie, and Gina as they
dove into the cookies.

"I'm starving," said Izzy.

"Me too," said Marie.

"Already?" asked Maddie.

"Sure," said Marie. "And anyway, it's always a good
time for one of Allie's grandmother's chocolate chip
cookies. Try one."

"Your grandmother *made* these?" Maddie asked as
she ate her cookie.

"Yup," said Allie, munching. "Doesn't yours?"

"Make cookies?" said Maddie. "No way. My
grandmother doesn't even boil water for tea."

The girls chuckled. It crossed Izzy's mind that maybe

Maddie was trying to compliment Allie. She was acting kind of human, which was disconcerting. Of course, Maddie didn't act human for long.

"Hurry up and brush your teeth," Maddie said bossily, after Izzy had finished her cookie and pulled out her floss. "Don't keep us all waiting."

As efficiently as she could, Izzy flossed, brushed her teeth using water from her water bottle, and rinsed with mouthwash.

"Gosh, Izzy," said Charlie, sympathetically. "Even after just one cookie, you have to do all of that?"

Izzy nodded. She couldn't say anything because her mouth was full of mouthwash.

Around the next bend, the hikers saw a rock even bigger than Mount Shipshape.

"*I'll* name this rock," said Charlie. "I'll call it 'Sleeping Camel,' because it has two humps at the top, like a Bactrian camel. And see that part that sticks out over the ocean? That's the camel's nose."

"I bet there's a great view from the top," said Marie. "Let's climb up."

"Stick together," said Ms. Martinez. "Follow me." She

led the way single file along the very narrow path that zigzagged its way up the side of Sleeping Camel. The path was not terribly steep, but it was kind of slippery from ocean spray, so they had to watch their footing. The climb was worth it, though.

"Whoa," breathed Izzy when they reached the top and walked out onto the camel's nose. The view was spectacular. It seemed to be limitless. On three sides, there was nothing but sea and sky and sun and sand. A cool breeze lifted Izzy's hair off her sweaty neck and softly sprinkled her face with spray. "Oh," she said. "This place is The Best, isn't it?"

"Mm-hmm," all the girls agreed serenely. They sat and rested for a while. Izzy was lulled into peacefulness by the sunshine, the breeze, and the expansive view.

"I feel like we are the only people on Earth," sighed Marie.

"Or in the whole universe," said Izzy. "We're a hundred million miles from the sun, and the next nearest star is over four light-years away. We're all by ourselves in space."

Charlie began to bend and twist herself into yoga

poses. Maddie stretched out on her back, her hands behind her head, eyes closed. Ms. Martinez shrugged off her backpack, took out her camera, and took photos of the view. Izzy slipped the Squad's composition book out of her daypack.

First, she finished the notes for one mystery:

- Make an Observation: Dr. Tamaki looked unhappy at the rec hall meeting, and at the beach, she and Ms. Martinez sounded unhappy.
- Form a Question: What is bothering them?
- Form a Hypothesis: It has to do with the "terrible shame" and "waste" and "loss to science" that can't be stopped and will "happen soon."
- Conduct an Experiment: In this case, more data is~was needed ~~before an experiment can be planned,~~ so I'll ~~took and listen~~ we looked and listened for clues. Gina identified surveyors' stakes, and Allie saw Ms. Martinez and Dr. Tamaki frowning at a developer's plat, or plan for construction at Camp Rosalie Edge.
- Analyze the Data and Draw a Conclusion: ~~To come!~~ Camp Rosalie Edge is going to be divided up and built on soon.

Then, Izzy wrote the steps in the Squad's
next mystery:

- Make an Observation: Camp Rosalie Edge is threatened.
- Form a Question: What can the S.M.A.R.T. Squad do to save it?
- Form a Hypothesis: The S.M.A.R.T. Squad can save Camp Rosalie Edge by finding something unique about it that must be protected.
- Conduct an Experiment: Look for a phenomenal phenomenon. Some ideas are: dinosaur bones; rare fossils; endangered animal or plant, like a special kind of orchid; wildlife habitat; natural feature, like underground cave; source of natural energy, like wind power; something human-made, like a grave or artifact or remains of a structure that should be in the National Register of Historic Places.
- Analyze the Data and Draw a Conclusion: ???

When she had finished writing, Izzy put the
composition book back in her daypack. After a few
minutes, she, Marie, Gina, and Allie walked away from

the Sleeping Camel's nose to explore its humps. Ms. Martinez followed them, her camera in hand and her pack slung over one shoulder.

"Look at this, Ms. Martinez," Gina said to her as she came closer. "The rock's split."

The girls were inspecting the space between the camel's humps, where there was a deep gash shaped like a sharp V with rough, rocky sides. It was as if a huge knife had sliced the rock in two, so far down that they couldn't see to the bottom. But Izzy could hear water swooshing where waves swept in and out under the camel's nose. At its top, on either side, the cavity was surrounded with slick rocks covered with damp moss and lichen.

"Wow, that's deep," said Ms. Martinez. As she bent over to look down into the space, her backpack slipped off her shoulder and tumbled into the abyss. "Oh, no!" she cried. She stepped forward, lost her footing on the slippery moss, and slid feet first into the gash, waist high. "Help! My legs!" she screamed. "All of you stay away from that edge!"

"Ms. Martinez!" shrieked the horrified girls. They

fell to their stomachs, reaching out to help her. Izzy yelled, "Charlie, Maddie, come quick!"

As Charlie and Maddie came running, Ms. Martinez struggled to wrench herself free, but it was no use. "I'm *stuck*," she wailed. "My legs are wedged between the rocks. I can't get out."

It flashed through Izzy's brain that if she took the S.M.A.R.T. Squad composition book out of her daypack right now, she would write:

- ◦ Make an Observation: Ms. Martinez has fallen into a cavity between rocks.
- ◦ Form a Question: How can we get her out?
- ◦ Form a Hypothesis:

For the first time ever, Izzy could think of nothing to write, nothing to try, nothing to do.

"DON'T MOVE, MS. MARTINEZ," said Charlie, kneeling at the edge of the crevice. Her voice was steady and calm. "You might only wedge yourself in more. Just take a deep breath, and when you feel ready, tell us and we'll try to pull you out."

"How did this *happen?*" asked Maddie.

"Her pack fell into the crevice and she stepped forward and tried to grab it and she lost her balance and slipped and now she's stuck," Marie said all in one burst, as if she were reciting a chemical formula.

Allie added, "The pack's a goner, washed out to sea probably."

"The satellite phone is in it," said Izzy shakily. "So, we can't call for help."

Maddie whipped her phone out of her pack and tried desperately to find a signal. "Oh, my phone is useless," she wailed.

"What will we *do?*" asked Ms. Martinez. Her voice was tight, as if she were struggling to sound calm despite her distress and pain.

Izzy felt terrible for mentioning the satellite phone and making Ms. Martinez even more upset. Suddenly, she realized: Acting anxious was not an option. Trevor's rhyme about the gravity of cavities was right. Ms. Martinez was stuck, and it was a grave problem. This was no time to freak out. It was time for action.

Izzy squatted next to Ms. Martinez. "Don't worry," she said in a reassuring tone. Gently, she patted Ms. Martinez's hand. "We'll get you out. You're going to be okay."

Then, swiftly, Izzy put her physics brain to work and came up with a plan. She turned to the others. "Charlie and Maddie, you two have the longest arms," she said. "Kneel on either side of Ms. Martinez. She'll put her arms over your shoulders. You put your arms around her waist. The rest of us will brace our feet and hold you from behind so you won't slip forward. You pull her and we'll pull you."

"Okay," said Charlie and Maddie. Both knelt without hesitation.

"Just a second," said Gina. "Izzy, you have the smallest arms. Maybe you could wiggle your hands down into the crack in front of and behind Ms. Martinez's legs to protect them as they're extracted. Her pants are all torn up, and we don't want her legs to get any more scratched or cut than they already are. What do you think?"

Snakes! thought Izzy. *That's what I think: There may be snakes hiding in that dark crevice.* But again, with an effort of will, she hid her fear. She nodded and said, "Sure, I can do that."

"Okay, good," said Gina. "Are you ready, Ms. Martinez?"

Ms. Martinez nodded. She put her arms over Maddie's and Charlie's shoulders. They wrapped their arms around her waist.

Gina held on to Maddie and Marie. Allie held on to Charlie.

Izzy lay on her stomach just in front of Charlie's knees. She wriggled her hands into the crevice, one hand in front and the other behind Ms. Martinez's legs. The sides of the crevice were jagged, so the backs of her hands were more cut and scratched with every inch, but she shoved them down as far as she could, which was only as far as Ms. Martinez's knees. "Everyone in position?" she asked.

The other girls nodded, and so did Ms. Martinez.

"Okay, then," said Izzy. "On the count of three. One, two, three. *Pull!*"

Charlie and Maddie leaned back, straining to lift Ms. Martinez, who closed her eyes and grimaced, biting her lip. It looked as if she was trying to stop from crying out in pain.

Izzy fought the urge to cry out, too, as her hands were getting crushed. Sharp rocks scraped and tore her skin.

The toughest part was hauling Ms. Martinez up enough so that she could sit on the edge. When she was finally seated, the girls took a break. Izzy tried to catch her breath. Then she and the others pulled again, Izzy guiding and protecting Ms. Martinez's legs past the knife-edged rocks; first her knees, then her calves, then her ankles, then finally, her feet. When Ms. Martinez was fully freed at last, they were all quiet for a second, panting from their exertion.

"Thank you," said Ms. Martinez in a hoarse whisper.

"You did really well," Izzy said to her kindly as she gave her water to drink.

"I'm going to look at your legs now," said Charlie. She had helped her moms in their veterinary clinic, so she knew how to evaluate injuries. "Tell me if this hurts." Very gently, Charlie felt along Ms. Martinez's legs from the knees down. Ms. Martinez winced, and her face was pale. When Charlie tried to move her right ankle, Ms. Martinez gasped, "Ouch." She jerked her leg away, a reflex reaction to the pain.

"Nothing's broken, thank goodness," said Charlie. "But I think your right ankle is badly sprained. I'm going to roll up your pant legs and look at your cuts and bruises now." Slowly, Charlie peeled Ms. Martinez's pant legs off her bloodied skin. Ms. Martinez tensed and shivered involuntarily.

"Your left leg isn't too badly hurt," said Charlie. "It just has scrapes and scratches. But your right leg has a bad gash on it, not down to the bone, but deep. It's bleeding a lot." She turned to the others. "All the cuts have dirt, sand, and little bits of rock in them. We don't have any antiseptic, so we're going to have to pool our drinking water to wash out the cuts as thoroughly as we can. Otherwise, they may get infected."

The girls rummaged in their daypacks for their water bottles.

"Wait," Izzy cried suddenly. "We *do* have antiseptic."

The others looked at her dubiously. She dug into her daypack, which was full of tooth-care supplies, and pulled out a bottle. "Mouthwash!" she cried. "We can use it to clean out the cuts. See? It says right here on the label: 'Kills germs and bacteria.'"

"In your mouth," said Allie. "But does it work on skin?"

Izzy handed the bottle to Charlie, who said, "It's worth a try."

"Actually," added Marie, "the same mixture as mouthwash was first used as an antiseptic for surgery.

Later, people figured out that it was good for cleaning mouths, too."

"This may sting a little," Charlie warned Ms. Martinez before she poured the mouthwash onto her scrapes.

Ms. Martinez nodded and closed her eyes. She shuddered, but she didn't pull her legs away.

When Charlie finished cleaning the cuts, she said, "We should really wrap the right leg in a clean cloth to stop the bleeding and keep the cut clean."

"Hang on," said Maddie. "I've got a T-shirt in my pack. I always bring extra clothes."

"I'll say," said Allie. "We saw your huge bags back at the cabin. Now we're glad you overpacked."

Maddie ignored Allie and handed a T-shirt to Charlie, saying, "Use this."

"Are you sure?" asked Ms. Martinez. Her voice was weak. "That's a souvenir tee from a rock concert."

"Yeah," said Maddie. She shrugged. "I broke up with the boyfriend who gave it to me, so, hey. No biggie to use it as a bandage." She pulled her bandana off and her green hair looked even greener in the bright sun. As she gave her bandana to Charlie she said, "You can use this to tie the shirt on her leg."

"Thanks," said Charlie. "That's nice of you, Maddie."

Izzy saw an unfamiliar expression cross Maddie's face: She looked grateful for Charlie's compliment.

Charlie dampened the T-shirt with mouthwash and used the bandana to tie it tightly around Ms. Martinez's right leg.

"Thank you," said Ms. Martinez. "That's better."

"Well," said Charlie. "This fix is only temporary."

"We need to get you off this rock and back to Camp Rosalie Edge as soon as possible," said Izzy.

"Right," said Charlie. "If you can stand, Maddie and I will help you move."

Charlie and Maddie helped Ms. Martinez stand. She wobbled, and the color drained from her face. Izzy was afraid her teacher would faint. But Ms. Martinez steadied herself, and with Maddie on one side and Charlie on the other, she was able to hop, using only her left leg.

Izzy and Allie led the way down Sleeping Camel, checking the path for obstacles. Gina carried Maddie's pack and Marie carried Charlie's. They brought up the rear, keeping an eye on Ms. Martinez, ready to catch her if she fell backward. The trek down took a very long time. The path was narrow and wet underfoot, so the going was treacherous. They had to stop often to allow Ms. Martinez to get her strength back.

At the bottom of the path, Maddie said, "We need to rest."

"Ahhhh," sighed Ms. Martinez as she sank to the sand.

The girls propped daypacks under Ms. Martinez's right leg to keep it elevated and also under her head to make her comfortable. Gina hurried upland into the woods. Izzy met her at the edge of the woods and helped her carry the three sticks she'd found. One was a tall stick that was wide at both the top and bottom. "For Ms. Martinez to use as a crutch," Gina said. "It's splayed at the bottom, so it won't sink into the sand. And here are two short sticks to make a splint for Ms. Martinez's right leg."

"Nice, Gina," said Izzy as they walked toward the others. "Good finds."

"Oh, sure, no problem," said Gina. She sounded subdued. "You know what? Just now, I saw more surveyors' stakes in the woods, like the ones Allie and I saw back at camp. That's evidence that the developers are planning to build here on Sir Pent Island."

More stakes, thought Izzy. *More reasons to solve the mystery, fast.*

Charlie and Gina put a short stick on either side of Ms. Martinez's right leg and wrapped the splints in place securely with a strap from Gina's daypack. As soon as Ms. Martinez said she was ready to move, the girls rose up, brushed the sand off their packs and their pants, and began to walk.

Izzy knew that they faced a long walk back to the boats and then a long paddle back to camp. But they had to keep moving; they had to bring Ms. Martinez back to camp for her safety, no matter how tiring the slog. Izzy was grateful to Allie, who, though surely tired herself, used her energy to bolster their spirits by singing as they walked:

Row, row, row our boats
Goodbye, Sir Pent Isle.
Off we go, back to camp, Cabin Two, here we come,
Pooped but with a smile.

They all took turns helping Ms. Martinez keep her balance while she was hopping forward. Her crutch was better than nothing, but it was cumbersome to carry and awkward to use on the sand. The sun, no longer overhead, shone directly into their eyes. Their pace was slow, and they stopped frequently because everyone was dragging, not only Mrs. Martinez. Izzy felt as though they'd *never* see Mount Shipshape, or the spot on the other side of it where they'd left the canoe and kayaks.

On one rest break, Allie announced, "Good news. I've got another cookie for everybody. Energy guaranteed. I promise you'll feel better after a giant chocolate chip cookie."

"Yes," said the girls, eagerly taking a cookie each.

"Kale chips for everybody, too," said Charlie, offering the open bag.

Everyone dug in with enthusiasm. Charlie's kale chips were not usually such a big hit, but Izzy was so hungry that she was grateful for Charlie's more-healthy-than-tasty snacks. From the way the others chowed down on the kale chips, Izzy could tell that they were hungry, too.

"I'm kind of sorry we won't be spending the night here on the island," joked Allie as she munched. "Because we won't find out if Maddie's dangerous hissing, screeching, grabbing creature haunts Sir Pent Island or not."

"I'm not telling," said Maddie, comically cramming her mouth full of kale chips.

Izzy laughed with the others, happy to hear Maddie playing along with Allie's joke. But Izzy had a sense of foreboding. Another danger, one that was real, was haunting her. It was a danger that threatened their plan—and Ms. Martinez's health and safety.

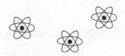

Earlier that day, when Ms. Martinez and the girls were full of energy and excitement, their hike from Mount Shipshape to Sleeping Camel had taken less than two hours. But now they were struggling to move their feet, and though Ms. Martinez tried as hard as she could, she could move only at a snail's pace.

Izzy's feet weren't the only part of her that felt heavy. Her heart sank when they rounded the bend and saw Mount Shipshape looming in the distance. Her worst fears were confirmed. The disaster on top of Sleeping Camel, caring for Ms. Martinez, and their very slow progress had meant that their return hike had taken them more than three hours. Now they were too late. It was high tide. Even from a distance, Izzy could see that water engulfed the pointed base of Mount Shipshape. Waves crashed against it and flowed far up the beach. The path they had taken earlier was completely underwater. The water was too deep to wade through. The waves were too strong to swim through.

Izzy tensed.

They were stranded.

7

"What?" asked Charlie.

Izzy pointed, and everyone looked at Mount Shipshape. Immediately, they realized what the problem was. They were cut off from the kayaks and canoe,

... and from all of their food,

... and their overnight equipment and supplies,

... and, worst of all, their transportation off the island.

"Oh, *no*," wailed Allie. "It's my fault. I should have done the math. Low tide at one p.m. means high tide at seven thirty p.m. It's nearly that now. I'm so sorry. If I had realized, some of us could have run ahead to get the boats."

"It isn't your fault, Allie," said Ms. Martinez. "I'm the one who slowed us down. Now we're stuck." She shook her head. "Even a landlocked poet like Emily Dickinson knew how dangerous it is to flirt with the tide." She recited:

What Skipper would
Incur the Risk
What Buccaneer would ride
Without a surety from the Wind
Or schedule of the Tide—

The Squad exchanged concerned looks. "Do you think Ms. Martinez hit her head in that fall, too?" whispered Charlie. "She's talking kinda crazy."

"No," Izzy reassured her. "Ms. Martinez quotes poets all the time. It's normal for her. Trust me."

Gina spoke up in a brisk, practical voice: "Probably someone will come and get us."

"No one back at Camp Rosalie Edge expects us to return until shortly after dawn tomorrow, remember?" said Marie. "No one will come looking for us. And we can't call for help because the satellite phone was in the pack that was swept out to sea."

Maddie took her phone out and tried again to find a signal, but it was no use. "I can't get this thing to work," she said, sounding panicky. "What'll we do?"

Izzy knew from years of Dizzy Izzy experience that panic wouldn't help anything. Trouble had to be treated the same way a scientific problem was treated: methodically, step by step. "The first thing we need to do is to make Ms. Martinez comfortable," Izzy said in the calmest voice she could manage. "Then we need to make a plan."

No one spoke. Instead, they nodded.

Izzy and Charlie helped Ms. Martinez walk to the near side of Mount Shipshape. The other girls trailed along behind them. At the base of the huge rock, Izzy took Ms. Martinez's crutch while Charlie helped her sit down in a shady, protected spot where the scrub trees met the sandy beach. Everyone else sank down, too, sighing with exhaustion.

Mrs. Martinez closed her eyes. "I'm going to rest," she said.

Izzy spoke quietly. "Let's apply the scientific method and work through our problem so that we can figure out what to do," she said. "The first step is Make an Observation. We observe that Mount Shipshape is too big for Ms. Martinez to climb up and over, and the point of its base is now surrounded by water. The water is too deep for any of us to wade through, and the waves are crashing against the rock with so much force that it's too dangerous for any of us to try to swim around the point during high tide."

"Add to that observation this data," said Allie. She glanced at her watch. "We have to wait six hours and thirteen minutes for the tide to be fully out. That means low tide is not until after one a.m., pretty much the middle of the night. Even if we stayed awake and walked around the tip of Mount Shipshape at low tide, we'd be walking in the dark and paddling back to camp in the dark, too."

"No way," said Maddie, and all the others murmured in agreement.

"The next step is: Form a Question," said Gina. "The obvious question is, What should we do?"

"Based on our observations, it's clear that trying to leave is too dangerous," said Marie. "My hypothesis is that the most sensible thing to do is spend the night here on the island. Agreed?"

"Yes," everyone nodded.

"Since we can't get Ms. Martinez back to camp until tomorrow, it'll be up to us to do the very best we can to take care of her leg," said Charlie.

"What needs to be done?" asked Maddie.

"Well," said Charlie. "Ideally, we'd build a fire, boil water to be sure it's clean, and use it to wash out her cut thoroughly. As long as we're boiling water, we might use some to make tea, because Ms. Martinez has lost blood, so she needs to keep drinking fluids, and also hot fluids are calming. Then we'd use a salve to soothe the scrapes on her skin. But …" Charlie counted their lacks on her fingers. "We don't have matches. So we can't have a fire. We don't have tea. And we don't have a salve."

Everyone sighed. "I'm afraid we'd Analyze the Data and Draw the Conclusion that we're sunk," said Gina sadly.

Then, Izzy had a brainstorm. "Nope. That's the wrong conclusion," she proclaimed. She grinned a huge grin, held up her daypack, and shook it so that it sloshed and rattled. "You're forgetting my mobile dentist's office. I've got almost everything that we need to start a fire and take care of Ms. Martinez's leg."

"You *do?*" asked Maddie.

Izzy nodded. "Allie, can you collect some dry leaves, twigs, and sticks? I'll need them to start the fire and keep it going," she said.

"Sure," said Allie.

"And Gina, can you construct a way to hang a metal water bottle over the fire so we can boil the water?" asked Izzy.

"Glad to," said Gina. "It'll be an engineering challenge."

"I'll gather pine needles for tea," said Charlie.

"That's a good idea," said Izzy. She handed Marie her tube of toothpaste. "I think you can use this non-gel toothpaste as a salve to soothe the scraped skin on Ms. Martinez's legs."

"I'll read the ingredients to be sure it has menthol in it," said Marie.

"I still don't understand how you're going to start a fire without matches," said Maddie, looking skeptical. "Do you have magic in that pack, or what?"

"I've got something much better than magic," said

Izzy. From her pack, she took her mini-mirror and waxed dental floss. She held one in each hand, saying, "I've got science."

Izzy squatted. Allie handed her dry leaves and twigs. Izzy put the leaves on the sand, then unrolled a length of dental floss and wrapped it around the twigs. She tilted the mini-mirror to reflect sunlight onto the leaves and after a few minutes …

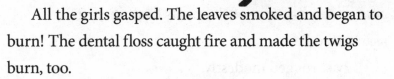

All the girls gasped. The leaves smoked and began to burn! The dental floss caught fire and made the twigs burn, too.

"Good job, Izzy," said Charlie.

Izzy blew on the tiny fire very softly. Carefully, she fed it more bits of dried leaves until it was going well enough for more twigs, then small sticks, then bigger sticks. When the small fire was burning steadily, Gina stuck two Y-shaped sticks on either side of it, added a stick as a cross bar, and hung her metal water bottle full of water from it. It took a while, but the water boiled eventually.

Allie used some of it to make pine needle tea. She woke Ms. Martinez and helped her sip the tea. Charlie waited for the rest of the water to cool a bit, and then she used it to thoroughly wash Ms. Martinez's legs and her bandages. Marie dabbed toothpaste on Ms. Martinez's cuts and scrapes, and then Charlie re-bandaged her legs.

"I cannot thank you girls enough," said Ms. Martinez. She smiled at Izzy especially as she said, "You are impressive."

"How do you guys know how to do all this crazy, science-y, seat-of-the-pants healing stuff?" asked Maddie.

Izzy shrugged modestly.

Allie grinned at Maddie and said slyly, "If Atom Middle School had a STEM team, you could learn how to do cool stuff like this, too."

Maddie held up both hands, palms flat, in surrender. "I hear you," she said, grinning. "Point taken."

Ms. Martinez drifted off to sleep, and the girls each had a sip of the pine needle tea. "This tea is okay," said

Charlie. "But I'm starving and we're all out of kale chips."

"And cookies," said Allie.

"I've been thinking," said Izzy. "It sure would be helpful if we had our big packs and the coolers with the food—"

"And drinking water," Marie added. "We really need it."

"I wish I could fly," said Charlie. "All that stuff is right on the other side of this giant rock."

Izzy nodded. "I don't know how big this island is, but I'm pretty sure it's too big for me to walk all the way around to get to our boats," she said. "It took us two hours to get as far as Sleeping Camel. But it won't be totally dark for another hour or so. I think I could climb up and over Mount Shipshape, pack the canoe, and paddle back."

Maddie squinted at Izzy. "Do you know anything about rock climbing?" she asked.

"Yes," said Izzy. "It's a tug of war between gravity and friction."

"If you know anything at all about climbing," said

Maddie brusquely, "then you know that you absolutely CANNOT go alone." She stood up. "I'll go with you."

Izzy and her friends were so surprised by Maddie's offer—bossy but kind—that they didn't speak.

Finally, Marie said, "I'll wake up Ms. Martinez and ask her if she's okay with your plan."

Marie knelt next to Ms. Martinez and shook her shoulder gently until she opened her eyes. After a short conversation, Ms. Martinez nodded.

Marie reported back, "Ms. Martinez says okay as long as two of you go. And be careful."

"Good," said Maddie. She went on in a very take-charge manner, "Charlie and Marie, you two need to stay and take care of Ms. Martinez. Gina, you need to tend the fire. Allie, you help Gina. Izzy and I—"

"Hey, wait," Allie interrupted. "Why can't I go, too?"

"Because you, Allie Oops, are the world's worst paddler," said Maddie.

"I was only pretending," Allie said. "I'm really good."

"Really good at pretending to be bad," Maddie said with a hint of a grin. "Anyway, the canoe will only fit two of us when we cram all our backpacks into it." Then she turned to Izzy and ordered, "Come on."

"Do you … do you know about climbing?" Izzy asked.

"I've been going to the climbing gym since before you were born," said Maddie. "Plus, I'm the tallest one here. And you need a tall partner because—"

"Because I'm Eeensie Izzy?" she asked with a twisted smile.

"Oh," said Maddie, sounding exasperated. "I shouldn't have called you that. I'm sorry. But you've got to admit: You're so small you could probably use some of that dental floss of yours as belaying rope, if we were belaying, which we are not. This is going to be strictly up and down, hugging the rock all the way. Let's *go*."

"Good luck," called the other girls kindly. Maddie led the way and Izzy followed.

There was no path up the side of Mount Shipshape as there had been up Sleeping Camel, but the rock face was not sheer. It was pitted with small cavities, good for toeholds and handholds, and also bumpy with small ledges and points that jutted out, good for grabbing. Maddie went first. Izzy soon saw that Maddie was a careful climber, and she appreciated her advice. "Put your left foot here," Maddie would say, or "This one's a good handhold." It required total concentration to climb; Izzy and Maddie had no time for any unnecessary talking.

Though both Izzy and Maddie were good climbers, they were panting when they reached the top of Mount Shipshape. They flopped down on their backs to rest. Izzy took slow breaths, trying to bring her heart rate back to normal.

"So, Maddie, I've got to say: You *rock* at rock climbing," Izzy said. "You're a good strategic climber, and you're strong."

"You're not so bad yourself," said Maddie. "But it's not only you ice hockey jocks that are in good shape. We figure skaters have speed, endurance, and power, too." Maddie paused. Izzy couldn't see her face, but she heard the sincerity in her voice when she said, "Listen, I'm sorry you and I got off on the wrong foot."

"The wrong skate, you mean," Izzy joked gently.

"I guess I did go all mean girl on you that day you tried out for the hockey team," Maddie said. "I was sure that you had no hope of making the team and that you'd get creamed by the other players because they were so much bigger than you. I was wrong, I mean, *really* wrong. You rule ice hockey."

"Thanks," said Izzy. She imitated Maddie. "I've got two things to tell you: One, you're a good climber, and two, I'm glad you are with me."

"I've got two things to tell you, too," said Maddie. "One, that guy Trevor, the one who likes you, is cute, even for a sixth grader. And two, don't blow it by being all self-conscious about him."

"We're only *friends*," Izzy insisted.

"Okay, okay," said Maddie as they stood up. "I'm just saying. You don't have to like him in a mushy, honeymoon kind of way, but he's good future-boyfriend material."

"*Arrggh*," groaned Izzy, covering her face with her

hands. "Talking about it is so embarrassing."

"Maybe now," said Maddie. She began to lead the way down Mount Shipshape to the beach. "Sixth grade is all drama, especially about boys. But it gets easier, you'll see. And as for embarrassment, that gets easier to handle, too. No matter how red-hot the embarrassment, a little time cools it off." She waved a lock of her green hair at Izzy and said dryly, "Trust me. I know what I'm talking about, embarrassment-wise."

"Listen," said Izzy earnestly. "We didn't do that to you. I promise. We didn't dye—"

"Whatever," Maddie cut her off. "All I'm saying is, just try to be normal around Trevor."

"Normal?" said Izzy.

"Yeah, on second thought, I guess normal is aiming too high in your case," said Maddie with a wry grin. "Well, you're smart. You'll figure it out."

Going down the far side of Mount Shipshape was easier than going up had been, which was good, because as the girls descended, so did the sun. As it sank lower and lower in the sky, the shadows on the rock became trickier. Izzy found it hard to tell if a ledge was a sturdy enough place to safely put her weight or if a shadow was making it look bigger than it was, in which case, a foot might slip, gravity would take over, and, *crash,* down she'd fall.

Maddie looked as relieved as Izzy felt when they landed safely at the bottom of Mount Shipshape, on the soft sand.

"Done," said Izzy. "Let's get that canoe loaded up while we can still see."

Wasting no time, Izzy and Maddie put on their safety jackets and helmets. They tucked the food cooler into the canoe behind the bow seat and squashed the packs in the stern. It was hard to drag the loaded canoe across the sand, but since it was high tide, they did not have to drag it very far to the water. Izzy hopped into the bow seat, and Maddie pushed off so that the canoe was afloat. Then she jumped into the stern seat.

The heavily laden canoe rode low.

"Good thing you're a featherweight," said Maddie to Izzy. "Otherwise, the water would come over the sides and sink us."

Though some waves did slosh over the sides, the

canoe did not swamp. They stayed afloat—barely. At first, the going was tough because Maddie and Izzy had to paddle into the waves. Spray splashed Izzy in the face, and her arms ached from digging deep and paddling hard. Still, when she looked ahead toward the blue line of the horizon and saw the sun melting into the sea, she was struck by how beautiful it was, how elemental, how mysterious, how *perfect*. She paused, lost in thought and wonder, thinking about how dependably changeable the sun, moon, and ocean were: They were eternally the same, yet constantly changing in their cycles.

"Hey, Popeye the Sailor Girl," Maddie called out to her sharply. "Get your mind back in the boat. This isn't the time to be distracted."

"Oops, sorry," Izzy apologized. She stopped daydreaming and started to paddle again.

Once they were past the point of Mount Shipshape, the canoers put their backs to the horizon and turned landward. The wind was behind them, so they paddled only to steer, while the waves propelled them to shore. As they came near, Allie, Charlie, Marie, and Gina ran down the beach waving their arms and greeting them with cheers.

"Ahoy!" they hollered. "You made it." They waded out to the canoe and beached it with Maddie and Izzy still aboard. "Welcome ashore."

"Did you enjoy your sunset cruise?" asked Charlie, helping Izzy climb out onto the sand. "You had us scared that you wouldn't be back before dark."

"Yes, thank goodness you're back," said Gina. She swung her big pack over her back and lifted the food cooler out of the canoe. "We're glad to see you and even gladder to see this food cooler. Allie was about to make us go fishing for dinner with toothbrushes as rods and dental floss as fishing line."

Allie laughed. "Now instead, we can use the dental

floss to make a clothesline over the fire, so Maddie and Izzy can cook their socks dry," she said playfully.

"Toasted socks for dinner?" said Charlie. "No thanks. I'm going to eat whatever the mess hall sent in the cooler, even if it's gelatin."

The girls carried their packs up the beach. Ms. Martinez said she was feeling much better, though she was still weak and achy. Charlie made sure that she drank plenty of fluids with her dinner and ate protein. All the campers ate heartily. Luckily, the mess hall had sent plenty of food: carrots, apples, tuna sandwiches, cheese slices, hummus, olives, almonds, and cookies.

"These cookies are okay," said Maddie, "but nowhere near as good as the ones your grandmother makes, Allie."

"Right," said Allie. She looked pleased—and surprised—by Maddie's compliment. Allie made a confused face that only Izzy could see, as if to say, *Who is this nice person who looks exactly like Maddie?*

Darkness fell and a gusty wind picked up. It blew the sand into the girls' hair and eyes. Allie and Marie put their arms over their heads, and Izzy hunched over to protect herself.

"Let's move off the beach," said Ms. Martinez. "We don't have to go far, but I think it'll be a good idea to set up our overnight camping spot in the woods. That way, we won't have to battle the windblown sand."

"Good idea," said Marie. "I'm so coated with sand that I feel as crunchy as a toasted sesame bagel."

The girls gathered their belongings. Gina dismantled the bars over the fire, and then Allie buried the fire in wet sand to be sure that it was completely out. Marie and Maddie each took one handle of the food cooler, and

Izzy carried Ms. Martinez's pack while Charlie helped her limp along on her crutch. There was no path, and they had only their flashlights to light the ground ahead of them as they made their way inland through the scrub brush.

They soon passed an eerie, marshy swamp with spiky reeds and dead branches sticking up out of the brackish water. Here and there, they saw ferns and pondweeds so unusually large that they looked like something out of a science fiction movie.

"This swamp is spooky," said Gina. "It gives me the creeps."

"Me too," said Allie.

"Hey, Maddie," said Marie. "This place is the perfect

setting for the ghost story you told at the campfire. You know, the one about the scary swamp creature that is part raptor, part snake and swoops low over its victims, screaming and hissing, and then wraps itself around them and drags them down into the muck and drowns them so that they are never seen again."

"I remember," drawled Maddie. "Allie reminded us just a while ago. You don't have to tell the whole story *again*."

"It's a good thing that creature's just pretend," said Izzy. She shuddered. "I hate snakes."

"Me too," said all the other Squad members—except Charlie, who didn't hate any creature.

They were glad to find a dry area good for their sleeping bags in the center of a small grove of trees. Gina made a shelter of branches for Ms. Martinez and spread her sleeping bag inside it. Charlie took the splints off Ms. Martinez's leg so that she would be more comfortable, and Allie made sure she had water to drink in case she woke up in the night. Ms. Martinez thanked the girls. Then she stretched out in her sleeping bag inside her cozy shelter and went to sleep.

The girls were worn out, too. They set up their sleeping bags like the petals of a flower with their heads facing in toward the center so that they could talk a while before they fell asleep. As she unrolled her sleeping bag, Izzy admitted to herself that the Squad's troubles and adventures had distracted them from their mission of saving Camp Rosalie Edge. Izzy thought over the list of things to look for: dinosaur bones, rare fossils, endangered animals or plants, wildlife habitats, underground caves, wind power, or human-made artifacts. These were all good ideas, but ... Izzy sighed. She and her friends had been far too busy to look, and they certainly had not stumbled onto any of them. That failure, crushing as it was, could not be helped. Their focus had to be on getting Ms. Martinez back to camp.

Izzy turned to the group. "We should go to sleep now, because we have to get up really early tomorrow. As Allie reminded us, the tide will be high again by seven thirty a.m. We'd better head to the kayaks no later than four thirty a.m."

"Fine by me," said Allie. She started to yawn, but just then, something flew by, right over the girls.

Izzy felt rather than heard it.

Allie sat up abruptly. "Was that a bat?" she asked, covering her hair with her hands.

"If it is a bat, you should be glad," said Charlie, "because bats eat mosquitoes."

"Well," said Marie, exaggerating, "I have so much mouthwash bug repellent on me, no self-respecting mosquito will bite *me,* and any one that *does* will have fresh, minty breath."

They all laughed softly. Then silence fell as they each began to drift off to sleep.

Hissss, Izzy heard. *Shriek.* And again, *Hissss.*

"Very funny, Gina," said Marie. "Okay, you've proven you can imitate the swamp creature. Now cut it out. I want to sleep, okay?"

An ear-splitting *screeeech* was the answer. Then again, Izzy had the feeling of a winged creature swooping by silently, close overhead.

"*Eeeek!*" shrieked the girls, frightened. Every single one of them bolted upright. Charlie and Maddie turned on their flashlights.

"*Whoa,* what was *that?*" asked Charlie in a hoarse whisper. "It's a good thing we're scientists who do not believe in monsters or I'd think we were being attacked by Maddie's swamp creature."

"Don't be silly," said Maddie. "That sounds like a barn owl."

"Don't owls hoot?" asked Izzy. "You know, like, *whoo, whoo?*"

"Well, barn owls hoot when they're mating," said Maddie, "but usually they shriek or squeak or tick or hiss."

"I didn't know you knew about birds, Maddie," said Izzy.

"You mean, you're surprised I'm not a total bird brain, right?" said Maddie.

"Nice one," said Gina. "I can see that you're catching

on to our cool punster vibe, Maddie."

"Arrggh," pretend-growled Maddie. "I knew it would be dangerous hanging out with you sixth graders."

"Seriously," said Izzy. "I'm impressed. It seems like you know bird stuff."

"Well," said Maddie slowly. "I like raptors. And barn owls are totally out-there. Like, their ears, for example. One is slightly higher than the other, and one opens up and the other opens down, so they can triangulate to locate their prey. And their hearing is so good that they can hear mice and voles and shrews under the grass."

"Do their prey hear them coming?" asked Allie.

"No," said Maddie. "Barn owls have special feathers and a special wing structure that allow them to fly silently."

"I like barn owls, too," said Charlie. "And I don't want to contradict you, Maddie, but barn owls aren't on the chart that Ms. Martinez gave us of the known birds on Sir Pent Island."

"Yes, I know," said Maddie. "And when I came on my Outdoor Ed trip when I was in sixth grade, no one ever mentioned barn owls on any of the islands. But that sure sounded like one."

"Well, how come we didn't see or hear any today?" asked Marie.

"Barn owls usually hunt at night," said Maddie. "In the daytime, they sleep so soundly that it's hard to wake them up." She paused. She seemed to be deciding whether or not to share something she cared about, something she was excited about. Excitement won. Maddie said, "I'm sure that *some* kind of owl lives on this island, though. Look what I found." Maddie pulled something out of her pocket. She shined her flashlight on what looked like a lumpy, irregular clump of compacted hair in her hand.

The girls leaned in to look.

"What is it?" asked Izzy.

"It's an owl pellet," said Maddie.

"Ick," said Allie, jerking back. "You mean it's the owl's poop?"

"No, and in fact, if you pick something up that looks like this but it smells, put it down and wash your hands right away," said Charlie. "Owl pellets don't smell, but animal scat does."

Maddie explained, "An owl pellet is fur and bones. It's the indigestible stuff that the owl coughs up. The owl eats its prey—mice, voles, and shrews—whole, but it can't digest the bones and hair, so it regurgitates them. If you pull this apart, you can see the bones of what the owl ate, like maybe the jawbone of a vole."

"That's even more disgusting," said Gina. "I can't believe you picked it up and put it in your pocket."

"Do you think this is a barn owl's pellet?" asked Marie.

"It could be," said Maddie. "It's the right size, about two inches long. And it's the right color, sort of blackish brown. There are no shiny insect remains on the outside, like other owls' pellets have. Barn owls eat insects only if necessary."

An idea began to simmer in Izzy's head. One of the ideas on the Squad's list of things to look for was phenomenal phenomena. Izzy asked, "Are barn owls endangered?"

"Not yet," said Maddie. "Though in some states, like Wisconsin and Connecticut, barn owls are in the category called vulnerable because their numbers are so dangerously low—and getting lower."

"How come?" asked Gina.

"People!" exclaimed Charlie. "Human disturbance. Barn owls are electrocuted by power lines, hit by cars, and get tangled up in barbed wire fences. As Maddie said, barn owls rely on their extra-sharp hearing to hunt, which gets totally screwed up by noise pollution from cities and highways. Also, people kill off their food supply by using rodent poison, and destroy their foraging habitat by building on it. Barn owls hunt in grasslands, wet meadows, and the edges of wetlands like that marsh we walked past earlier, and when those places are developed, the barn owls starve."

"People are destroying their nesting sites, too," said Maddie. "Barn owls don't build nests. They lay their eggs in dark, hollowed-out spaces, surrounded by pellets. The same space is used year after year, by different barn owls. They use natural nest sites, like tree cavities, or other birds' nests."

"Then why are they called barn owls?" asked Izzy.

"Because they also nest in human-made cavities, too, like nooks and crannies in barns, abandoned buildings, and chimneys," said Maddie. "All those sites are harder and harder to find—impossible, really, when farmland is paved over and wild places are turned into parking lots." Maddie paused, "Izzy why are you asking so many questions?"

"Oh, I'm just curious," Izzy said. She tried to sound casual, even though her idea was so good that it made her heart beat faster and her words pour out in a rush. "Like, what if there never were barn owls someplace before, like let's say here, on Sir Pent Island, but now there are owls here because the place the owls used to live got developed and so the owls had to move here so they could hunt and nest? Wouldn't that mean that their new home had to be kept safe for them? I mean, like, protected from development?"

"What are you getting at?" asked Maddie.

The S.M.A.R.T. Squadders were quiet.

Izzy could feel their unspoken question—*Should we tell Maddie?*—crisscross and hop from one to the other. The silent answer was *yes*.

Allie glanced at Ms. Martinez as if to be sure she was soundly asleep. Then she burst out in an intense whisper,

"We're pretty sure Camp Rosalie Edge is going to be destroyed. We found evidence that it's going to be divided up and built on by developers."

"Oh," Maddie gasped. "Now something makes sense. On the first day at camp, before I came up to Cabin Two, I saw a truck parked behind the rec hall with the words 'Ace Construction and Development' on its doors. I thought it was weird, but now I understand. Oh, this is *terrible*."

"Yes," said Izzy. "So do you think the presence of barn owls could stop development?"

"I don't know," said Maddie. "If we found a species of barn owls that was endemic—that existed *only* here— then that would make a difference. Because if their habitat were destroyed, that would be the end of them. And there are a lot of barn owl species found only on small islands like this one."

"Even if the species of barn owls here is not endemic, I think there's still hope," said Charlie, speaking softly. "Because as Maddie said, barn owls are on the vulnerable list in at least two states."

"Lots of people love owls," Marie added. "I bet if we

got the word out to birders that there are owls on Camp Rosalie Edge property, they'd protest the development of this area."

"Well, I think we all agree that Izzy's idea about owls saving camp is worth a try," said Allie. "It's a hypothesis worth exploring. So, we have to follow the scientific method, like we always do, and treat this situation just like the other mysteries the Squad has solved."

"Allie," cautioned Charlie. She held her finger in front of her lips and tilted her head toward Maddie to stop Allie from spilling the beans about the S.M.A.R.T. Squad and ruin its strict policy of secrecy. No one outside the Squad was supposed to know about it or the mysteries the girls had solved at Atom Middle School.

But it was too late. "Soooo," said Maddie, crossing her arms over her chest. She kept her voice low as she said, "I'm picking up that you guys have some kind of secret society, like an undercover science sleuthing club, where you use your scary smartness to solve mysteries. I saw how you applied the scientific method before, to figure out what we should do. Now you're applying it to saving camp. You're, like, the Brainiac Bunch, aren't you? Isn't that right?"

The other girls exchanged sidelong glances. "Well," Izzy began. "We—"

"Never mind," said Maddie. "Don't get all bent out of shape. I understand: You sort of started a renegade STEM team, which is typically weird of you, but freakishly cool. Hey, hang on. Are you the ones who solved the air-conditioning mystery back when school was freezing all the time? And did you also figure out why everyone was getting sick in the library—that mold problem?"

No one spoke.

"Okay, I get it, you took a vow of silence," said Maddie. "Your secret is safe with me." She grinned and swept her fingers over her chest, saying, "Cross my heart."

"Ahem," Izzy cleared her throat. "Back to the owls. So, the first thing we have to do is prove there are barn owls here. Maddie's got her pellet, and that might be good evidence. But I think we have to *see* an actual owl. Tell us what they look like, Maddie, so we can go find one."

"It's not that easy," Charlie began. "First of all, it's pitch-dark. We can't find an owl—"

"Not if we don't look," Allie interrupted. She was already standing up and putting on her shoes, and so were Gina, Marie, and Izzy. "But we do need to know what we're looking for. Give us the scoop, Maddie."

Maddie stood up, too. "A barn owl has a white heart-shaped face and long, feathered legs and long wings that fold behind its tail," she said. "It looks goldish-brownish from above and white from below, with some white feathers on its chest and black polka dots all over."

"Oh, so cute," said Marie.

"Maddie, it's out-there how much animal stuff you know," said Gina.

"Oh, yeah," said Maddie in an offhand way. "I've been interested in birds, and crustaceans, too, from way back. When I was a little kid, I kept a crab leg, saved from dinner, in my room. It reeked after a day or so, but I wanted it as part of my crustacean collection."

"Way to go, Maddie," laughed Izzy.

"Anyway, so I think the best place to start looking is where I found the pellet," said Maddie. "Come on. I'll show you. Hurry up!"

Silently, because they didn't want to disturb Ms. Martinez, and gingerly, because there was no path, the girls picked their way through the woods. Maddie led them back to a tree they had passed on the way to their camping spot. Back then, Izzy had not noticed what she saw now: The tree had a cavity in it that was deep, though not very long or wide.

"Look," said Gina. She bent over and pointed her flashlight on pellets at the base of the tree.

"Oh, do the pellets mean that a barn owl is roosting in this tree?" whispered Allie, looking up into the crevice.

"Maybe," said Charlie. "Probably. And see this white stuff on the trunk? That's owl poop, which is also a sign that an owl lives in the tree cavity."

"I never thought I'd be so excited to see poop," giggled Gina.

Charlie knelt down and picked up a pellet. "You know," she said. "People sell owl pellets to schools and labs so students can dissect them. Knowing there are pellets here might add to the argument not to develop camp, or at least Sir Pent Island. Camp wouldn't make a lot of money selling pellets, but it might make some. Let's bring back samples."

Charlie knew the proper way to collect the pellets to bring back to camp safely. She lifted each one carefully and put it in its own clean little paper napkin, which she had saved from dinner.

"Don't collect too many pellets," said Maddie. "Take only a few. I've read that the natural owl pellet supply is limited. Also, if owls are using this tree, their nesting area shouldn't be disturbed."

"It's too bad we don't have a camera," said Marie. "Then we could take photos of the tree and the pellets."

"Oh, my camera works," said Maddie. She waggled her cell phone. "I don't have a cell signal, so I can't make a call. But I can take photos."

"So, Maddie," said Izzy. "First you're a climber. Then you're a birder. Now you save the day with your camera. You are as full of surprises as an owl pellet. And I mean that as a compliment."

"Okay, I'll take it," said Maddie.

After Maddie took photos of the tree and the pellets,

the girls sat on the ground and tried to stay as quiet as possible, hoping to see an owl return to the tree cavity. After a while, Izzy struggled to keep her eyes open and her legs felt heavy with fatigue.

"My foot's asleep," Gina sighed. "I feel like we've been here *forever*. I don't think the owl is ever going to show up."

"We must have scared it away," said Izzy. "Probably it's shy."

Charlie asked, "Should we try to find another tree with a cavity in it and pellets at its base?"

"And white poop on its trunk?" added Gina.

"I'm really sorry, but I vote no," said Marie. "I think we'd better go back to our camping spot and check on Ms. Martinez to be sure she's okay."

"And we should try to get some sleep," said Allie. "We have to be up and ready to go by four thirty a.m., or we'll miss low tide again and be separated from the kayaks."

"But we can't give up," said Izzy. "What about our idea of finding a phenomenal phenomenon to save camp?"

"We're not giving up on that," said Gina. "We have the pellets and the photos of the pellets and poop. That's not proof of owls, but it's evidence."

Everyone except Izzy stood up, stretched, yawned, and turned back toward their camping spot.

"Come on, Izzy," said Maddie. "You can't stay here by yourself."

Slowly, reluctantly, Izzy stood. She sighed and then followed along, a few steps behind Maddie. Just before it was lost from view, Izzy turned to take one last look at the tree, and …

9

Izzy reached out and grabbed Maddie's arm, and then pointed to the tree.

"Oh," gasped Maddie, with a sharp intake of breath, which made all the other girls stop and turn. They gasped, too, because there, perched on a branch next to the cavity, was a barn owl.

The owl lowered its head and swayed from side to side. No one even breathed. They were transfixed. The barn owl was smaller than Izzy expected. Moonlight lit its white heart-shaped face and the white feathers on its chest. Its feathered legs looked long in proportion to its body. The owl's wings were folded and the tip of its tail showed just below the branch. Izzy had never seen anything like it. The owl seemed to have come from

another world entirely, solely for the purpose of showing itself to the girls.

Silently and deftly, Maddie pulled her phone from her pocket. They all knew that the flash and click of the camera would frighten the owl away, but the photos had to be taken. The owl stopped swaying for a moment, and in that instant, Maddie took as many photos as she could before the owl, in one swift and silent swoop, flew away.

For a moment, all the girls stood absolutely still. Then Allie spoke for them all, saying in a voice full of awe, *"Whoa."*

Izzy's knees felt weak. The group waited a minute or two, but the owl didn't return, so they walked back to their camping spot silently, but each with a bounce to her step.

Izzy was sure that she was too excited to sleep, but she must have drifted off, because the next thing she knew, the alarm on Maddie's phone was beeping and Allie was shaking her awake.

"Time to go, Izzy," Allie said cheerfully. "We don't want to be stranded here because of high tide again."

"That's right," said Ms. Martinez, already up and

at 'em. "Yesterday we learned firsthand the truth of the poet Geoffrey Chaucer's words: 'Time and tide wait for no man.'"

"Okey dokey," said Izzy. She rubbed her face and rose up. The sun was not yet above the horizon, but the sky was lighter at the edges, promising a bright blue sky day.

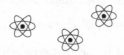

After a quick snack of granola bars and apples, the campers packed up. Ms. Martinez said that she was feeling much better, but Charlie insisted on cleaning the cuts on her legs again and re-bandaging the biggest scrape on her right leg before they left. Gina made her a new crutch, though she had to walk only as far as the canoe, which was still beached where the girls had left it after Izzy and Maddie's sunset paddle the evening before. Maddie and Allie dragged the canoe to the water. Izzy helped Ms. Martinez put on her safety jacket and helmet and climb in.

"I can paddle," Ms. Martinez said. "My arms are fine."

"No, you're the passenger today," said Allie as she fastened her own safety jacket. "And since I'm the best paddler, I'll power the canoe from the stern, and we'll put Maddie in the bow."

"You?" asked Maddie, pulling on her helmet. "Miss Crash-'n'-Splash? The best paddler? I don't think so."

Allie looked a little sheepish. "As I told you earlier, I was teasing you yesterday," she admitted. "But that was before you turned out to be not so awful after all."

Maddie put her nose in the air and pretended to be miffed. "Watch out," she said. "My not-so-awfulness is nearly used up."

Allie and Maddie paddled out to deeper water, but stayed close to shore as the other girls began their short and easy walk to the kayaks. As it came in, the tide lapped the shore, but there was still a fine, though narrow, path on the sand around the pointed tip of Mount Shipshape. The girls put their gear in the kayaks, fastened their safety jackets and helmets, and pushed off. Gina and Izzy paddled their red kayak right behind the canoe, and Charlie and Marie followed them in their blue kayak, bringing up the rear.

Allie sang,

Row, row, row our boats
Splashing all the way,
Bringing good news to Camp Rosalie Edge, we think
We have saved the day.

As the sun rose and burned stronger, so did Izzy's determination. She dug her paddle into the water, making her strokes deeper and faster, eager to return to camp. The S.M.A.R.T. Squad and Maddie had some work to do before they could find out if Allie's song was right.

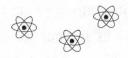

Of all the islands, Sir Pent Island was farthest from the main part of camp, so even though Izzy and the Cabin Two crew had a predawn start, some of the other sixth graders had already returned from their overnight trips. They were unloading their gear from canoes and kayaks onto the beach by the time Charlie and Marie pulled the blue kayak ashore next to the other Squad boats.

Trevor came over to help. When he saw them, his

eyes got big. "Uh, are you guys okay?" he asked.

"Sure," said Izzy, puzzled by his expression and his question. Then she realized: They must be quite a sight, what with Ms. Martinez hip-hopping along with one leg in a splint made of sticks and her crutch made of a branch, Maddie with her green hair looking slick and shiny and stuck to her head when she took off her helmet, and the rest of them dotty with non-gel toothpaste dabbed on their scrapes and bug bites. Izzy laughed. "I guess we look pretty rough," she said. "We had a wild trip."

Trevor laughed, too. "I can't wait to hear all about it," he said. "I'll save the seat next to me on the bus so you can tell me on the way back to school."

"Okay," said Izzy cheerfully. "That'll be good." She was proud of herself. Usually, she would be hot with self-consciousness about looking so crazy. But she knew that Trevor was totally nonjudgy, and after all she'd been through the past 24 hours? *I don't give a hoot how I look,* she thought, grinning at her own owl-y pun. She wouldn't be able to tell Trevor about finding the owls, but wait till he heard about Ms. Martinez falling in the crack.

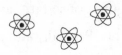

Later in the morning, the Squad and Maddie were gathered in Cabin Two. Charlie was just back from delivering Ms. Martinez to the camp's first aid station.

"Will Ms. Martinez be okay?" Izzy asked.

Charlie nodded as she chewed and swallowed a bite from an apple as big as a volleyball. When she could talk, Charlie said, "The camp nurse said Ms. Martinez's leg is going to be fine, thanks to our quick and thorough care." Charlie grinned. "The nurse was totally blown away by how we used mouthwash as a disinfectant."

"I would have gladly scrubbed myself head to toe with disinfectant," said Marie as she emerged from the bathroom with her head wrapped in a towel. "I told those crickets and spiders to move over. I invaded their space and took a shower. Oh, it feels great not to be gritty."

Marie and Charlie joined the other girls, who were squashed together on Gina's bunk, huddled over Maddie's phone, feverishly researching barn owls.

"What have you guys got so far?" asked Charlie.

"Well, we found the 1918 Migratory Bird Treaty Act and the 1973 Endangered Species Act," said Gina. We're hoping those laws will protect the barn owls we saw."

"And we found out that owls are apex predators," said Allie. "That means they're at the top of the food chain, and any change in their habitat messes up the whole chain. Like, if people kill weeds, then the bugs that eat those weeds die, then the rodents that eat those bugs die, and then the owls that eat the rodents die."

"We're trying to figure out if the barn owls on Sir Pent Island are a unique species. All of us JCs have permission to use the camp office," said Maddie. "So I went there and downloaded the photos from my phone onto the camp computer and printed them on the office printer." She held up her hand to stop Charlie's question before it was asked, saying, "Don't worry. Nobody saw

me." Then she went on, "We're using my photos to compare the physical traits of the barn owl we saw on Sir Pent Island with other barn owl species. We're hoping the species on Sir Pent Island is found only there."

"It's driving me crazy not to have my laptop," Allie complained. "The screen of Maddie's phone is so small that it's too hard to see details, so we can't be sure."

"Maybe instead you should look up local bird registers," suggested Marie. "And call local birding clubs and ask about the barn owls they have seen."

"Those are good ideas," said Izzy, "and we can suggest them to Dr. Tamaki. But I'm afraid all we can do right now is the most basic research."

"We only have to come up with enough facts and questions to give Dr. Tamaki a place to start further research," Charlie reassured her, "and reasons why the developers can't start building until a proper biological study is conducted."

"How are you guys in the Big Brain Club going to handle this?" asked Maddie. "Are you going to blow your top secret cover and tell Dr. Tamaki what we found?"

"No," said Gina. "We're always anonymous. We like it that way."

"So let me get this straight," said Maddie. "You're not going to claim the fame you deserve?"

"Nope," said Izzy. She held up the S.M.A.R.T. Squad's

black-and-white composition book. "We'll do it our signature way: I'll write a report. I'll pull out the pages, and we'll put the report and your photos and the owl pellets on Dr. Tamaki's desk without her seeing us." Izzy paused. "I hope you don't mind, Maddie," she said. "You deserve some of the fame, too. A lot, actually. If we stood up in front of everybody and told about our discovery, you'd be a hero. That would be great for you, because I know that you love this camp."

"And I know that you do not love going public, especially making speeches," said Maddie. "Keeping our news quiet is okay with me. I think it's kind of cool to be part of a secret." She gathered up the printed photos and handed them to Izzy, saying, "Here, go ahead and add these to your report."

"Oh, the owl is so gorgeous," said Izzy as she looked at the photos again. "Thanks, Maddie. These photos are The Best." She grinned. "Like I said, you're a rock climber, a birder, and a photographer. Nice."

"And even more proof that you'd be a great asset to a STEM team," said Charlie, smiling.

Maddie blushed, pleased. But in typical Maddie

fashion, she said, "Don't get carried away. I prefer the figure skating team. But I am going to tell my mother to tell the school board that Atom Middle School should have your STEM team."

"Thanks," said all the girls, high-fiving.

"Speaking of science," said Marie, "we did two experiments to prove to you that we did not dye your hair green. The pool water did."

"Wait, what?" asked Maddie.

Allie ran to the bathroom and returning, held up the baggie containing the clump of her hair floating in pool water. "The copper and chlorine in the pool water turned my blond hair green, too," she said. "Just like yours."

"It's sort of the same reason these copper pennies turned green when we put acidic vinegar on them," said Marie. "I'm afraid you'll need chelating shampoo to get the green out."

Maddie shrugged. "Whatever," she said. "I have two things to tell you: First, I think my green hair is rad. You know I'm into birds, and when my head is wet, it looks like a male mallard's head. I'm not in such a hurry to undo it now." She sounded truly apologetic when she said, "And second, I'm sorry I blamed you."

"Well, you know us," said Allie. "We like solving tough scientific mysteries."

"The hairier the better," quipped Izzy, looking up from writing her report. "That pun came right off the top of my head."

Everyone groaned, especially Maddie. "I am going to go spend time with the other JCs," she announced. "I need some intensive eighth grader–ness to counter-balance all this Cabin Two–ity. I'll see you guys at lunch."

10

The S.M.A.R.T. Squad stopped at Dr. Tamaki's office
on their way to the beach for a swim before lunch. Izzy
slipped inside as the other Squad members kept watch.
She put her finished report, illustrated with Maddie's
photos, on Dr. Tamaki's desk and weighed it down with
two owl pellets. As she did so, she made a fervent, silent
wish, *"Let this work."* She knew her friends felt the same
way, because when she emerged, they held up their
hands with all their fingers crossed. Izzy held up her
crossed fingers, too, and then they all ran as fast as they
could, down the road, across the beach, and straight into
the ocean.

It felt great to Izzy to dive in. Allie bobbed up,
buoyant, next to her and said, "I bet Dr. Tamaki is going

to read our report any minute now."

"Maybe," said Gina, treading water nearby.

"We're putting a lot of pressure on cute little barn owls," said Marie, floating on her back. "It's a big job to save a whole camp."

"I really hope the owls on Sir Pent Island are their own species," said Charlie, who was so tall she could stand on the sandy bottom. "Then everybody will be concerned about protecting their habitat."

Izzy, also floating, listened to Charlie's words, but her heart and mind were focused on the papers she had left on Dr. Tamaki's desk. Would her report make a difference? She could only hope so.

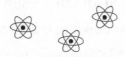

The girls were early to lunch at the mess hall, partly because they were starving. It had been a long time since their small and hurried breakfast on Sir Pent Island. But they were also early because they couldn't wait to see if anything was going to happen because of their report and if so, what.

At first, the answer was, nothing.

"I can't believe I'm actually impatient for the gelatin to come," said Gina. "I'm hoping that Dr. Tamaki is waiting until dessert to make our announcement."

"We'll see," said Izzy. She was unable to eat any of her lunch. Her stomach was too fluttery.

Finally, when they had almost given up hope, Dr. Tamaki stood and clapped her hands for attention. "We'll be loading the buses in about one hour," she said. "Pack up and clean up your cabins and then come back down to the rec hall. Ride in the same bus you came in. We're sorry to see you go. You've been a great group."

"At-om, At-om, At-om!" the students chanted.

Dr. Tamaki clapped for quiet again. "In fact, Atom Middle School will go down in the history of Camp Rosalie Edge," she said. "Someone from your school, in this very group, has probably saved our camp from being destroyed." Dr. Tamaki paused dramatically, and then said, "Developers wanted to divide the camp property and build on it."

A wave of murmurs swept the room. None of the S.M.A.R.T. Squad members looked at any of the other members, but they linked hands under the table, and squeezed hard when Dr. Tamaki said, "But just in the nick of time, someone put a report on my desk this morning. Whoever wrote the report did not say which island they went to on their overnight, but they found barn owls there. They took photos, and they brought back pellets as proof. We have already made some calls and we'll investigate further, but the new presence of barn owls on our property may well save our camp. Let me say thank you to the Atom Middle School sixth graders who discovered this and wrote such a fine report."

The mess hall erupted in cheers and whoops. "Way to go, Atom Middle School! Yay, Camp Rosalie Edge!"

Izzy looked across the mess hall at the junior counselors' table. Maddie gave her a half smile, so quickly that if she'd blinked, Izzy would have missed it.

"You know what's great?" said Allie, as the Squad walked back to Cabin Two after lunch. "Since the camp will probably stay open, we can come back and be junior counselors when we're in eighth grade, like Maddie did."

"That *is* great," said Charlie. "That means we don't

have to say goodbye to Camp Rosalie Edge, only see you later."

All too soon, it was time for the girls to depart. As the Squad lined up to board their bus, Dr. Tamaki said, "I'm glad you campers from Cabin Two went to Serpent Island. I must say I was surprised when you chose it. Most kids don't want to go there because it has so many snakes."

"WHAT?" gasped the girls.

"You didn't see any?" asked Dr. Tamaki. "There are big snakes there. That's why it's called *Serpent* Island."

"We thought it was Sir Pent Island, S-i-r P-e-n-t," spelled Allie.

"Oh, I guess you never saw the name written down," said Dr. Tamaki. "It's S-e-r-p-e-n-t. SER-pent. You know, as in snakes."

"I wonder if Maddie knew and didn't tell us?" said Marie.

"Too late now," said Allie. The five girls collapsed against one another, laughing.

"*Sssssssnakessss,*" hissed Allie.

Izzy laughed so hard that she practically fell into the bus seat next to Trevor.

"It seems like you and your friends had a pretty exciting time," said Trevor.

"Yup," said Izzy. She smiled a mile-wide smile, not even thinking about her braces, and said, "We *always* do." She thought to herself, *It's because we're the S.M.A.R.T. Squad, The Best at Solving Mysteries And Revealing Truths.* "So, Trevor," she said. "Let me tell you what happened on our overnight. Remember that joke you made about the gravity of cavities? Well, Ms. Martinez fell into this huge cavity in a rock, but luckily I had all my mouth-care equipment, because …"

- Make an Observation: Camp Rosalie Edge is threatened.
- Form a Question: What can the S.M.A.R.T. Squad do to save it?
- Form a Hypothesis: The S.M.A.R.T. Squad can save Camp Rosalie Edge by finding something unique about it that must be protected.
- Conduct an Experiment: Look for a phenomenal phenomenon. Some ideas are: dinosaur bones, rare fossils; endangered animal or plant, like a special kind of orchid;

wildlife habitat; natural feature, like underground cave; source of natural energy, like wind power; something human-made, like a grave or artifact or remains of a structure that should be in the Historical Register.

- Analyze the Data and Draw a Conclusion: The S.M.A.R.T. Squad—and Maddie Sharpe—discovered the new presence of barn owls on Serpent Island. The owls may be on other camp property, too. Therefore, it is highly likely that the camp land cannot be developed. Therefore, Camp Rosalie Edge is saved from the developers. Therefore, it will stay open for years—and lots of sixth graders—to come!

THE TRUTH BEHIND THE FICTION
THE LAW OF CAVITIES

The S.M.A.R.T Squad encountered a lot of challenges at Camp Rosalie Edge. During the girls' Outdoor Ed trip, they had to face high tides, find birds in the dark, research complicated laws about migration and endangered species, and show how an oxidation reaction turns pennies green. Talk about Solving Mysteries And Revealing Truths! Read on to find out the facts behind the story.

TIDES, THE MOON, AND GRAVITY

Tides are the rise and fall of water levels in seas and lakes. At high tide, the water level is at its highest. At low tide, the water level is at its lowest. Even though the moon is 238,900 miles (384,500 km) away, its gravity is strong enough to slightly pull at the water in Earth's oceans and seas. This pull causes the water to bulge out on the side of Earth closest to the moon, causing what we call high tide. Meanwhile, another high tide occurs on the opposite side of Earth. This one is caused by Earth's spinning. The two high tides pull water away from all other oceans, and that's what causes two low tides.

HOW TO TURN PENNIES GREEN

1. Try to find pennies with copper in them. That means looking for U.S. pennies dated before 1982. Before 1982, pennies were 95 percent copper and 5 percent zinc. Since 1982, pennies are 97.5 percent zinc and 2.5 percent copper.
2. Line up the pennies on a paper towel.
3. Use a bottle cap or tablespoon to carefully place a drop of distilled white vinegar on each of the pennies.
4. Fold the towel over the pennies, and put them in a warm spot.
5. Wait at least 24 hours.
6. Look at the pennies. They should be GREEN.

WHY ARE THE PENNIES GREEN?

The vinegar is acidic. When acidic vinegar reacts with the copper in the penny and oxygen in the air, a blue-green compound called malachite is formed. This is called an oxidation reaction.

You can see a giant-size example of oxidation reaction: the Statue of Liberty. The statue is made of copper and started out a shiny copper color. It turned blue-green because of oxidation.

THE TRUTH BEHIND THE FICTION

BIRDING

Izzy and the S.M.A.R.T Squad find themselves looking for birds. You can, too. You don't need any special equipment to be a birder, but you do need to be able to:

Stop—or at least move slowly and quietly, whether you are trying to find birds in the city or the wilderness. All birds can see and hear you coming, but owls have the widest range of hearing and also exceptional vision. Stay still. Wait and observe.

Look—Many birds are camouflaged. That is, their coloring blends with their environment, which makes them hard to see. Try checking out a bird guide from your local library, or finding a book at the bookstore, to help identify these winged beauties. There are many excellent books that come with hundreds of photos to help you learn the name of the bird you have spotted, or about its habits, nests, and other characteristics.

Listen—Birds chirp, whistle, caw, shriek, click, and hoot. You can learn to identify a bird by the sounds it makes. Ask an adult to help you find websites that have sound recordings of birds' noises. Can you imitate the birds' sounds?

Barn owl

Robin

180

It's also fun to keep track of the birds you have seen. Birders do this using life lists, which name the birds they've spotted and/or heard. A birder's entry names the bird, the place, the date, and the time. Charts can help you identify found feathers, or bird tracks.

No matter where you are in this great big beautiful world, you might catch sight of a bird swooping by through the sky. But as free as they seem, birds face dangers from humans and from our actions. Thanks to the hard work of individuals and governments, laws have been passed to help protect our fine-feathered friends.

ENDANGERED SPECIES

The **Migratory Bird Treaty Act (MBTA)** is an international law that began in 1918 to protect birds that migrate, or travel, between Canada and the United States. Governments and companies must pay fines if they do not take steps that help keep birds safe from harm, such as making power lines easily seen by migrating birds and covering oil pits with nets. The MBTA has helped save millions of birds from injury or worse. Because of this act, the snowy egret, the wood duck, and the sandhill crane were saved from extinction.

Although the MBTA helped many birds, one treaty alone was not enough. In 1973, the U.S. Congress passed the **Endangered Species Act (ESA).** This law's goal is to protect all kinds of wildlife. The ESA makes it illegal to "harass, harm, or hunt," or "import, export, take, possess, sell, or transport" any living thing whose numbers are so low that they are in danger of becoming extinct, or disappearing forever. It also makes it illegal to destroy ecosystems, places that an organism needs in order to survive. There are over 1,300 different species in the U.S. listed as endangered or threatened, including species that may surprise you. Did you know that there are some types of squirrels, orchids, mice, cacti, bats, spiders, and clams on the endangered or threatened lists?

The loss of even one plant species—any species, in fact—can affect an entire food chain. For example, if people use pesticides to kill weeds, the insects that feed on those weeds will suffer and their population will decrease, and the birds and frogs that eat those insects could get ill, too, as will the larger animals that eat the birds and frogs, such as foxes, snakes, and owls. That's why protecting these endangered species and their entire ecosystem, is crucial to their survival.

How do you know if an animal you love or one you are studying is in need of help? You can find out the level of protection it needs by looking to the International Union for Conservation of Nature (IUCN). IUCN has identified seven levels of conservation: least concern (LC), near threatened (NT), vulnerable (VU), endangered (EN), critically endan-gered (CR), extinct in the wild (EW), and extinct (EX). As a

EX

Golden toad

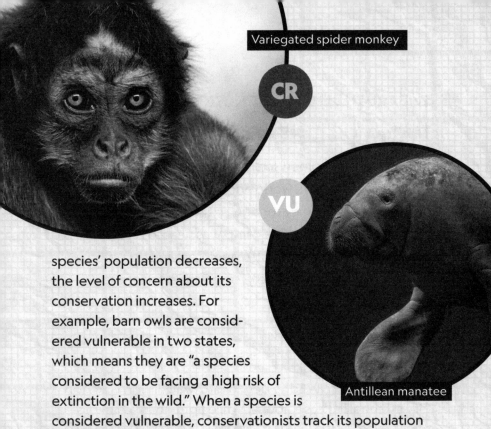

Variegated spider monkey

CR

VU

Antillean manatee

species' population decreases, the level of concern about its conservation increases. For example, barn owls are considered vulnerable in two states, which means they are "a species considered to be facing a high risk of extinction in the wild." When a species is considered vulnerable, conservationists track its population and the health of its habitat in the hope of increasing its numbers.

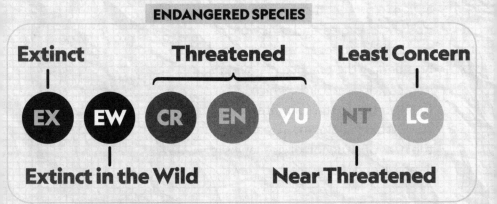

ENDANGERED SPECIES

Extinct   Threatened   Least Concern

EX   EW   CR   EN   VU   NT   LC

Extinct in the Wild   Near Threatened

WOMEN SCIENTISTS

The work of women scientists in the past and present has changed the world and will have a lasting impact on our future. You may recognize the name of the first woman listed below. (The camp was named after this pioneering conservationist!) Meet Rosalie Edge, a leader in her field, and two young women scientists at work today.

ROSALIE EDGE CONSERVATIONIST

Born in 1877, Rosalie Edge began bird-watching in New York City's Central Park as a hobby. While fighting for women's right to vote, Edge learned valuable lessons that helped her when she became a dedicated conservation-ist later in her life. Before Edge took action to protect them, raptors like goshawks, eagles, and owls were routinely killed for sport. Edge was horrified by the practice of paying hunters for dead birds, which led, for example, to the slaughter of 70,000 bald eagles in Alaska and the near destruction of goshawks in Pennsylvania. Edge created Hawk

Rosalie Edge with a red-tailed hawk

184

Mountain Sanctuary, the world's oldest sanctuary, or safe place, for birds of prey. She was instrumental in the creation of Olympic and Kings Canyon National Parks and prevented logging in forests adjacent to Yosemite. These parks protected the bird's unspoiled, safe habitats. Strong-willed and outspoken, Edge was fearless and unstoppable when it came to fighting for species preservation. All her life, with relentless conviction, she pushed organizations such as the Audubon Society to do more to protect species like raptors, and pushed even harder to convince the general public that protecting nature and the environment is everyone's responsibility.

BÁRBARA FREITAS
BIOLOGIST

Not every scientist is able to study a newly discovered species, but that's just what Bárbara Freitas is doing. Focused on a species of owl on Príncipe Island, which is found off the west coast of Africa, she studies the owl's genetic information, song, color, shape, and body structure, with the hope of learning as much as she can about this new bird. She also aims to understand what

Bárbara Freitas with a new species of owl discovered on Príncipe Island

the owl needs from its environment by figuring out how many live on the island and observing its habitat. Freitas has been passionate about birds since she was young.

NOELLE CHOAHNNA GUERNSEY
WILDLIFE ECOLOGIST, CONSERVATIONIST

Are you wild about wildlife? Noelle ChoAhnNa Guernsey is, too. A conservationist and ecologist who enjoys the natural world and learning about wildlife and healthy ecosystems, Guernsey earned a B.A. in ecology and evolutionary biology at the University of Colorado at Boulder. She spent several years working with habitat restoration for a variety of birds and mammals, making sure they had safe and healthy places to live. She later earned a master's degree in biology, and now works with Native nations to restore plains bison and black-footed ferrets in the Northern Great Plains. Guernsey hopes her work will help connect people to the natural world, diversify the field of natural resources in the United States, and engage youth in conservation efforts.

Noelle ChoAhnNa Guernsey holds a black-tailed prairie dog that she moved to a wildlife conservation area.

186

S.M.A.R.T. TERMINOLOGY

Does the idea of a confounding variable confound and confuse you? From apex predators to Newton's Law of Universal Gravitation, the S.M.A.R.T. Squad and their stories introduce you to complicated concepts and phrases. Here are some definitions to help you understand the ideas clearly.

APEX PREDATORS

Owls and other raptors, orcas, and big cats like lions and tigers are **apex predators,** which means that in nature, no other animals hunt them. They are at the top of the food chain. Any effect on the ecosystem can affect an apex predator's health and population numbers. For example, owls eat mice and other rodents that eat seeds from weeds and grasses. Killing weeds with chemicals means less food for these small animals and, in turn, for owls and other apex predators. Apex predators help keep an ecosystem in balance, too, because their hunting controls the size of their prey's population.

Orcas are apex predators in their food web.

CONFOUNDING VARIABLE

When you do an experiment, you change the **independent variable,** and you measure what happens to the dependent variable. Put another way, the independent variable is the *cause* and the **dependent variable** is the effect. For example, let's say that you want to see if sunlight helps an apple tree grow. You'd plant one apple tree in a sunny spot and another apple tree in a shady spot. The independent variable is the amount of sunlight each tree gets. The dependent variable is how big the trees grow. But sometimes in an experiment, there are other variables, called **confounding variables,** that can have an effect on both the independent and dependent variables. What? Well, in other words: There may not be enough water for the tree in the sunny spot, for example (that would be the confounding variable), which would lead you to draw the *wrong* conclusion about the effect of sunlight on apple trees.

ENDEMIC, EXTINCTION

The word **endemic** means that a plant or animal species is native to, or lives only in, a specific place and nowhere else in the world. For example, wild kangaroos are endemic to Australia. This is an important concept in conservation, because if a plant or animal is endemic to an area, that area can be protected, as can its habitat, in order to prevent **extinction,** which means its complete disappearance from Earth.

NEWTON'S LAW OF UNIVERSAL GRAVITATION

In 1687, Sir Isaac Newton wrote that gravity is universal, which means that all objects are drawn, or pulled, to each other with a force of gravitational attraction. And the closer the objects, the stronger the force. The farther apart the objects, the weaker the force. So, for example, the pull of gravity is stronger between two soccer balls when they are one foot (0.3 m) apart than between the same two soccer balls when they are three feet (1 m) apart. The way Newton stated the law is this: "Any two bodies in the universe attract each other with a force that is directly proportional to the product of their masses and inversely proportional to the square of the distance between their centers."

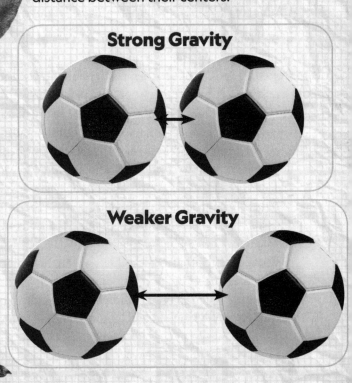

Strong Gravity

Weaker Gravity

ACKNOWLEDGMENTS:

In 2001, my friend, the poet Mary Clare Powell, sent me her poem "Things Owls Ate." It begins:

The sixth graders are dissecting them,
regurgitated refuse, indigestible parts
of things owls ate, found where owls roost,
near the white splash markings on barn boards.
The kids say the idea is gross but once they cut
open the hard shells it is soft gray feathers
and hair they first find. At the center of
that bed the bones appear, scapula and tiny skull.
The children are excited to match bone to
bone, using a printed guide, laying out the
frames of tiny eaten things. They learn anatomy.

That quiet poem stayed tucked in my brain for 20 years, waiting to spark the idea for *Izzy Newton and the S.M.A.R.T. Squad: The Law of Cavities,* a story about owls, and how there are surprises hidden in people and places, just as there are in owl pellets. Mary Clare illustrated for me the metaphorical link between fact and fiction, nature and human nature. My lovely and generous friend Kay Taub gave me an owl pellet of my own to dissect, much to my delight, and a printed guide to learn from. Clearly, generosity is abundant in people who love owls. Bárbara Freitas and Emma Gesiriech, both raptor experts, graciously answered my owl questions with expertise and enthusiasm and came up with even better ideas to bring authenticity to the story. My daughter Katherine, another owl fan, helped me tremendously by recollecting with good humor and specificity her memories of dealing with dental braces and her sixth grade outdoor education experience. We laughed and laughed, and all the while, Katherine was providing me with valuable pages of notes. Katherine's professional research and writing about the benefits of outdoor education for middle school students was an inspiration—as Katherine herself *always* is!

My friends Betsy Randall-David and Sara Jarvis sent thoughtful, thorough lists and, during our video call, generated a treasure trove of games and activities for Camp Rosalie Edge, all tried and true from Camp Lala-Gigi, which they created for their lucky grandchildren. Essential to my story were Betsy's and Sara's observations and insights about children's interactions and behaviors while camping. Mary-Grace Reeves, my pen pal since she was a little girl, has just graduated from Stanford Medical School. It was exhilarating how Mary-Grace immediately understood the idea of science affecting girls' friendships and came up with the funny, smart, and *perfect* idea of hair turning green from oxidation, which I loved. Once again, my trusty Lunch Bunch girls were the source of my story's heart and soul. With a combination of hilarity, dismay, and happiness, the girls talked about camp memories like crushes, gelatin for dessert, creepy-crawlies, ancient showers, and ghost stories. Thank you, Arsema, Baeza, Caroline, Emily, Madelyn, Morgan, and Nora, and your wonderful, gifted teacher Emily Pacconi, for your intelligence, kindness, humor, and steadfast friendship from sixth grade all the way to graduation, despite the pandemic. You are the personification of hope and potential. Becky Baines thought up the great title: *Izzy Newton and the Law of Cavities*. Thank you, Becky! Shelby Lees and Erica Green are my partners in joy in creating the S.M.A.R.T. Squad stories. I can never thank them enough for asking the question that brought all the elements of this story together:

What if Izzy has braces?

CREDITS: Background doodles throughout: Shutterstock and Adobe Stock; 180 (LO RT), Ger Bosma/Getty Images; 182, Michael and Patricia Fogden/Minden Pictures; 184, Hawk Mountain Sanctuary Archives; 185, Martim Melo; 186, Courtesy of Noelle Guernsey

The publisher would like to thank Jennifer Szymanski for her scientific expertise. The publisher would also like to thank Shelby Lees and Erica Green, editors; Julide Dengel, senior designer; Sarah J. Mock, senior photo editor; and Anne LeongSon and Gus Tello, associate designers.